SQUATTER'S GOLD

BOOK 1:
SAM WHITE HOMELESS MYSTERIES

Timothy A. Brown

For Walter and Marita Brown, loving parents who sacrificed much so that I would have greater opportunities.

SACRAMENTO CITY, Ca.

FROM THE FOOT OF J STREET

SHOWING I J & K ST WITH THE SIERRA NEVADA IN THE DISTANCE

"Homelessness is a humanitarian crisis that weighs heavily on our collective social conscience. Sacramento is blessed with an extraordinary and committed service provider community and we are working together to ensure that homelessness need not be hopelessness."

– Mayor Darrell Steinberg.

Prologue - Curse of Gold

August 4, 1850
Fifty miles east of Sacramento in the
unorganized territory of California, near the
upper Mokelumne River

M ichael O'Connor cinched up the belly strap on his donkey, carefully centering the heavy load. Prospecting tools, clothing and camp gear covered the twin iron strong boxes full of gold. The gold alone weighed about 25 pounds by his reckoning. His gold— the gold he had sluiced out of streams and dug out of the earth for a year in the steep backcountry—was collected in an oaken rack built by native Miwok. His brown and gray donkey was short and stout. He had named his donkey Pat, after a stubborn old ship's captain. Captain Pat had taken young Michael under his wing at the age of sixteen, had tutored him and treated him like a son.

O'Connor was of English and Irish descent and

hailed from Boston. He had been orphaned at sixteen and put to work on a whaling boat. He grew into a strapping young man and a skilled sailor who worked hard and caught on quick. After five years Captain Pat had made him First Mate for scores of commercial sailing ventures. He had sailed much of the Atlantic Ocean and the North Sea and his last voyage had taken him 15,000 miles around the tip of South America, then north through the Pacific Ocean to San Francisco Bay. At the age of thirty-one he left his life as a sailor to try his hand at prospecting gold.

He had sailed into San Francisco Bay just months after Sutter's gold discovery in 1849. He was among the first Argonauts (a term applied to 49ers who had come by sea for the California Gold Rush). In truth, he hadn't come for the rush. He was working on a ship on his way to California when the word got out. First Mate O'Connor had built up a sizable stake while working for long periods at sea, and had decided to risk it all on the search for precious metal.

When the treaty of Guadalupe Hidalgo was signed in 1848 and California was ceded from Mexico to the United States, there were just over seven thousand settlers. In

1849 alone over sixty thousand people flooded into the state.

His red mule Beet stood equipped with flanks rippling. He checked his saddle, slipped his arm and shoulder through his rifle strap, then mounted. He was leaving the claim that he'd worked for a full year. He had survived rain, snow, gun shots, skunks, bears, hunger, and mosquitos to name a few. He had developed the habit of talking to himself out in this lonely frontier and said out loud, "Michael O'Connor, you are one in a thousand." He smiled wide, and his gapped front teeth glinted in the morning sun through his thick mustache. "Thanks be to God, I finally hit the motherlode. Ma and Pa would be proud."

He gazed up into the heavens as if Katie and Kevin O'Connor were in the clouds smiling down on him. Then he shuddered and said to himself, "It ain't worth a pirate's fart until I cash it in. I got a long haul and dangerous waters to sail through." He made the sign of the cross. He sweat profusely on this hot summer morning and, wiping off his hairy face and neck with a rag, he set off down the trail. Pat the donkey followed behind Beet through a series of steep and treacherous canyons.

Still, he felt the warm glow that a rich man must feel when he doesn't have to worry about the next meal or where his future is headed. He had stashed in his saddle bag two pounds of gold dust that would cover the expenses of his trip and his stay in Sacramento. He would soon be buying new clothes, the best horse he could find, and some prime ranch land. Gold was used as currency in the mother lode country, but he knew that flashing his treasure around could make him a target, so he had to play a smart hand with a poker face.

O'Connor had started his prospecting foray with two donkeys and more tools than he was carrying out. He had been smart, buying his animals and tools in San Francisco rather than Sacramento where Samuel Brannan and other merchants gouged the miners for basic supplies. Squatter camps had sprung up as miners whose motherlode had not panned out ended up in town looking for work and couldn't afford the high rents.

He had traded with Miwok in his area for food, and other things he needed. He owed much of his success and survival to his relationship with the Miwok. When he'd first come to the area he had happened across a miner who had shot a teenage Indian boy and taken his sister, a young woman, as a prisoner.

The events of that day were etched in his mind. He rode over the hill the afternoon he'd arrived by mule a year earlier. He saw for the first time the same beautiful creek and canyon he had just left.

Gun shots had rang out that day—his donkey had bolted and his mule shook and stopped in its tracks. In a meadow below him he'd spotted the miner, a big man, pointing his smoking rifle in the direction of the young Indian boy, about a hundred yards away on the ground, squirming. The girl was tied to a tree in the miner's camp.

The miner seemed to be aiming the rifle for another shot at the boy who was already clearly incapacitated. Without time to think it over, O'Connor had slid his 'Mississippi' rifle off his shoulder and yelled down to the man, "Hold off! The boy's already shot." The surprised miner fired his rifle at the boy again, but missed. Then reloading and cocking his rifle, he turned to fire at O'Connor. O'Connor felt the bullet whiz by his left ear before he heard the shot and then he cocked, shouldered and fired at the miner who teetered and toppled. A halo of blood pooled around his head while his legs spasmed for ten long seconds.

O'Connor couldn't believe he'd hit the man, much less killed him, but the bullet had passed through the miner's thick neck and ended his life. O'Connor, still shaken, had untied the girl and treated the boy's leg wound as best he could, then wrapped him in his blanket. The girl led them to the Miwok camp in a larger river valley a couple miles away and the boy, who turned out to be the head man's son, survived his wound. The head man led a party of young men and O'Connor back to the site of the shooting and witnessed the miner's body.

Between a few words of English and hand gestures they conveyed that the miner had been a bad man who had fired on them whenever they came within sight. They helped him bury the body. With their approval O'Connor took over the miner's sluice operation. He found a few pounds of gold the miner had stashed in his half-built cabin and became a friend of the Miwok. The brother and sister he had rescued visited him from time to time and they exchanged bits of each other's languages and traded goods.

After two and a half days on the trail he reckoned he was less than ten miles east of Sacramento not far from the American River. O'Connor had managed to stay away from cities for a whole year and had mixed feelings about returning. He dreaded the noisy, crowded city and the boomtown prices, though some comforts like decent food, drink, printed news, conversation and warm accommodations definitely appealed to him. He'd passed a steady stream of miners loaded to the gills and looking for that special spot.

Most of them asked him how he'd done and he'd lied with a sad look on his face, saying, "I found a little dust, but mostly bust." If asked for advice on where to head he'd say, "You don't want to go where I've been, if you want to find gold that is."

He'd been wary of bandits along the road, having heard a number of accounts of hold ups by passersby, but he'd made it most of the way without a problem. It was about noon and he was still on the trail when a couple of dusty, disheveled men slouched out of the bushes about sixty yards ahead of him. They held pistols and looked dangerous, but drunk. He felt the hair on the back of his neck stand up and he quickly slipped his rifle off his shoulder. He couldn't spot any horses, so it looked like they were on foot, but he wasn't going to outrun anyone on his mule with his donkey tied on.

One of the unsteady bushwhackers slurred, "Two of us, one o' you, what say you leave us this donkey and ride on by with your mule and your life."

O'Connor thought his odds were pretty good given how inebriated these men appeared. He said, "You really ready to die just for my mangy donkey?" They were pointing their pistols in his direction and he pointed his rifle at the man who'd done the talking. "I may not get both of you, but I will kill you."

The two robbers glanced at each other and the talker nodded and fired. O'Connor quickly raised his rifle and fired as a shot zipped by to his right. He hit the lead drunk in the leg. Another bullet hit the dirt at his mule's feet.

The drunk he hit was on the ground yelping and the other took off into the brush, abandoning his partner. He fired again in the general direction of the fleeing drunk then yanked the mule's reins, yelled at his donkey and headed into the high brush. Another shot hit a tree nearby. He fired again and gained some distance riding away from them to the North.

He didn't think they'd pursue him with one man

wounded, but he kept moving away from the main trail to where he guessed the American River would be. About two miles further he thought he smelled the river and coming over a rise he saw the meandering green water like a king garter snake flowing west. He decided to wait until the next day to approach Sacramento. He followed the river west for a mile or two and found a small, concealed clearing near the river bank for his camp and thought hard about how to handle his gold.

At the edge of his camp, O'Connor sat with his back against a cottonwood tree bent by the river when it flooded each spring. He was cleaning his US model 1841, .54 caliber "Mississippi Rifle" polishing the walnut stock and brass fittings. It was the finest rifle available in San Fransisco and he had paid dearly for it. It had been named after the Mississippi Regiment that used it to good effect during the Mexican American War.

He watched the sun go down, the sky ablaze with red and orange clouds that were reflected in the green water. There were some sandy beaches ringed by thick trees and brush and a beaver slapped its tail on the water as it grew dark. He looked up through the leaves of the twisted tree and noticed a clump of bees a third of the way up the thickest middle branch.

Hundreds of bees were flying to and from a good sized hole. O'Connor suddenly had an idea. He had raided beehives for honey during his year in the gold country and wasn't afraid of them if he took precautions. He shimmied up the middle branch and climbed out onto a cross branch where he could get a look at the hive. The entry hole seemed to recede into the big branch a ways.

The light had turned from silvery gray to a dark navy blue when he returned to the tree. This young tree was a survivor, bent but not broken. Its twisted trunk and three branches reminded him of a giant trident. He sat on the bent trunk of this tree about three feet off the ground, his two metal boxes of gold on his lap.

Each box was a bit longer, but narrower than a cigar box. He'd burned his name and the year on strips of deer hide which he'd placed in each box. He removed three large nuggets from one of the boxes to take with him in case it took him a while to return. Then he placed a box into each side of his saddlebag. Doubt rose in his mind about his plan, but he couldn't trust his new found fortune to a merchant's safe and he couldn't come up with a better idea.

He started a small fire and later rolled a large piece of charcoal into his metal pot. He tied the pot to his saddle bag, which was hanging off his shoulder and tied around his waist. He donned his gloves, pulled his hat low and climbed the tree using branches that took him up face to face with the beehive. Moving slowly he secured himself and freed his hands. The hole looked perfect, with just enough room to stash his boxes.

Pulling a handful of green grass from his pocket, he placed it on the coal in the pot and blew the smoke into the hive to calm the bees. He removed the boxes from his saddlebags and carefully set each box into the hole, stacking one on top of the other.

On August 8, he rode his mule down the hot dusty streets of Sacramento at midday. O'Connor saw how much the city had grown in the year he'd been gone. More men arrived each day to try their luck as a growing number of disheartened 49ers were giving up and moving back into town. The merchants and landowners were the ones thriving in the boomtown. Sacramento was built on the confluence of the American and Sacramento Rivers. O'Connor had heard that both rivers flooded badly in January and forced many of the squatters to give up their low lying camps, which must have been a hardship for many in the dead of winter.

Construction of new levies had begun along river banks and canals downtown with crews of men happy to have work. He passed a new Methodist church being built and came to a temporary Catholic church under a large tent topped with a wooden cross on 7th and K Streets. There had been a large fire in April and charred buildings were also being reconstructed using more stone and brick than wood. O'Connor tied his mule and donkey to a rail by a water trough and sauntered into the Catholic tent where he saw a priest speaking to a group of people.

He waited until he could introduce himself, saying, "Father, I'm Michael O'Connor. I've been in the hills for a year and I'd like you to hear my confession please."

"I'm Father Augustine Anderson, God Bless You! And welcome to our humble church, which I hope someday becomes a cathedral. I have a confessional set up in back if you'll please follow me out."

They both sat in tiny spaces just big enough for a chair and darkened by thick burlap bags tied together as walls and ceilings.

O'Connor began, "Father, I have shot two men, one who tried to rob me and was wounded and one who I saw attack an Indian boy and girl, fired at me and was killed when I fired back. I didn't mean to kill him, but I did. I have been driven by greed to search for gold, but thanks to God I have worked hard and done very well and I pray to live in peace and to start a family, Amen."

Father Anderson replied, "Repeat after me the Act of Contrition. In the name of the Father, Son and Holy Ghost …" O'Connor recited the words following Father Anderson who continued, "I assign you penance of two Rosaries."

O'Connor thanked Father Anderson, made a generous donation in gold dust and offered, "Father, when you are ready to build a church, I would be glad to help."

The priest said, "We are drawing plans for our beautiful church as we speak my son, and would welcome your assistance."

O'Connor found lodging and livery and the next day, after a shave and haircut, he bought some new clothes. Now that he could relax for a spell he decided to grab a beer in McDougal's Saloon. While he drank his beer, he read the local paper—the *Placer Times*—to catch up on the news of the day. His ability to read had been crucial when he landed in San Francisco over a year ago and studied everything he could about gold prospecting and mining.

The front page story was about a group of leaders of the California Territory meeting in San Jose and designating counties as government entities within California. This group of leaders planned to petition the Federal Government for California statehood.

He also read about the squatters or "Free Soil" movement under the leadership of a Charles L. Robinson, which had challenged the right of speculators to throw squatters off their land. John Sutter held the original Spanish land grant and sold most of it to a small number of speculators. The squatters, some of whom had fought for the United States in the Mexican-American War, pointed out that since California was no longer part of Mexico the existing land claims were no longer valid.

He thought about how lucky he was and about finding the ranch of his dreams in this new land and pictured himself with a strong and beautiful woman working beside him. O'Connor's solitary life had been reduced to simple survival and daily gold mining for a year and he felt a bit overwhelmed by the speed of change around him. How different Sacramento had become in just a year!

The next morning O'Connor walked the downtown, scouting assay offices to see which were paying the most for gold. He found the differences amounted to a few cents, per ounce, but he was used to counting pennies. He also asked about horses for sale. He passed a number of noisy gambling establishments that hadn't been there when he had arrived. He reckoned that gambling was the last thing he needed. He thought of the young woman he had met in San Francisco, Anne Casey, who worked at her father's saloon. Her laugh, even his memory of it, warmed him inside and made him smile. *Once I'm a man of property and means, I'll go looking for Anne. God I hope she's not married.*

He entered an assay office at Second and J streets that seemed reputable and had a competitive exchange rate. After waiting his turn, he pulled out three gold nuggets and set them down on the counter. They weighed four pounds and at nineteen dollars, ten cents per ounce, he walked out with over twelve hundred dollars in his pocket and headed for the livestock market. After looking carefully at a number of horses, he decided on a roan stallion the color of chestnuts. He judged it to be among the best horses in the market and he began to dicker about price, which was wildly inflated by East Coast standards. He knew he paid a steep price at fifty dollars, which included a saddle and other necessary tack, but he was a proud man as he rode out of the market on his new horse, his head held high. He had dreamed of this moment so many times during the past year.

O'Connor spent the next two days exploring the outskirts of the city looking at properties. He'd hoped to find a nice spread with at least a small cabin that was no more than a day's ride into town. The perfect spot would be near a river or creek, but on high ground so as not to flood frequently. His dream was to plant orchards of fruit trees with room enough for his livestock to graze and provide him a regular source of meat and income.

On the second day he found a fifty acre property that seemed to fit his bill. It was north of Freeport, a small hamlet on the Sacramento River. He hoped he still carried enough cash and gold to make a down payment. If the owner accepted his offer he'd ride out to get the rest of his gold or at least enough to purchase his ranch. He could hardly contain his excitement to realize the dream for which he had worked so hard and risked so much.

On the eleventh of August he rode back into town and saw printed hand bills from the Free Soil Movement that charged speculators with "BRUTE FORCE." A Free Soil Meeting had been called for that evening on the levee. He was curious about this movement and headed toward the levee to find a couple hundred men gathered.

Charles Robinson introduced himself, called the meeting to order and delivered a rousing speech about how the greedy speculators and monopolists were trampling their rights and threatening violence. The angry crowd of desperate men were loud, rowdy and raunchy in their response to his message. Robinson then turned to a group of leaders in the organization and introduced two of them as James McClatchy and Richard Moran who were starting a newspaper for the squatters called the *Settlers and Miners Tribune* and they were roundly cheered.

Robinson then introduced squatter John T. Madden who had lost his court case the day before and was being threatened with eviction by the authorities. The rowdy squatters pounded the levy planks with their feet and rifle butts. One of them called out, "Over my dead body he'll be evicted." There was a roar from the crowd.

Next Robinson introduced Joseph Maloney as a veteran of the Mexican-American war and the leader of the squatters' militia. Maloney bellowed, "Step up and be counted! Join the Militia! Defend your rights and your brothers! Let's put up a fight if a fight is what they want." About half the squatters signed up right on the spot.

O'Connor thought to himself, *If I'd come back without any gold I'd be joining up right now, but I don't have a horse in this race.* The men passed several hats around and he made a $20 contribution to the cause, which turned a few heads. He got back on his horse and rode away, wishing the squatters luck.

On August twelfth he met with the seller of the Freeport property, but they drove a hard bargain, and would not come down at all from the high asking price. He told them he'd think it over and get back to them soon. He was disappointed—he really liked the property. He'd known he would have to contend with high prices for a place close to town, but it was the most important purchase he'd ever considered and it might be the biggest decision of his life. He thought, *I'll mull it over for a couple days before I decide.*

The next afternoon O'Connor went into McDougal's saloon, ordered a beer, a whiskey, and the night's special meal of elk steak and potatoes. He savored his beer and looked up to see a tall, broad-shouldered man standing over him.

Joseph Maloney extended his hand and said, "I remember you from the meeting a few days ago. Someone said they saw you drop twenty dollars into the hat. How come you didn't join my militia?"

O'Connor introduced himself and explained, "I'm sympathetic with your cause, but I'm not squatting myself and I'm fortunate enough to be buying my own property."

Maloney said, "Oh I see, you're one of the lucky ones who actually found some gold." O'Connor just smiled, shrugged and ordered a beer for the big man.

Over a couple of beers Maloney filled him in on the latest developments. A couple days after Mayor Harlan Bigelow promised not to prosecute the squatters, his Sheriff Joseph McKinney arrested James McClatchy and

Richard Moran for inciting violence through their *Free Soil* newspaper. They'd been shackled and taken to La Grange, an old boat formerly named "Stafford" that was anchored in the river and used as a jail.

Maloney said, "They've thrown down the gauntlet now and we have to respond. Look out tomorrow, things might get a bit testy."

O'Connor made the sign of the cross. "I'll pray it doesn't come to that my friend." They shook hands and bid each other good night.

On the morning of August fourteenth the town buzzed with gossip about the squatters who were arrested and how their militia had been summoned. The Mayor and Sheriff were busy organizing their own force and rumors got back to the Sheriff that the squatter militia was fifty men strong and they planned to spring McClatchy and Moran from the prison boat.

O'Connor was having lunch near Fourth and J Streets and thinking about his purchase of the Freeport property. He had decided that, even with the high price, he would go ahead with the purchase. This was his future, after all, and he felt it was worth the money.

He had just finished his meal when he saw over

forty men approaching slowly down Fourth Street, most armed and on horseback, in military formation. Others marched behind, some holding only swords or pitchforks.

Bystanders moved fast to clear the streets or cheered them on. He got up and moved out on the street smiling and waving in support of the "Free Soil" militia as they passed by on their way to La Grange. Maloney nodded to him as he rode by. He followed at a safe distance behind them, but when they came to the docks they found Mayor Bigelow, Sheriff McKinney, and their posse dug in directly in their path.

The Mayor yelled, "You all know I'm the Mayor and this here is Sheriff McKinney with appointed deputies and in the name of the law I'm ordering you all to stand down and turn over your arms here and now."

But Charles Robinson certainly wasn't going to give up that easily. "We ain't done nothing yet except exercise our right to bear arms and I thought you worked for the people, not the speculators! Free our brothers and we'll stand down" The militia men roared their agreement.

The Mayor yelled, "This is your final warning, lay down your weapons!"

Maloney of the squatters said to his men, "Shoot the Mayor if he moves on us, but let's retreat strategically for now." The squatters turned around and started back up from where they came. He watched them walk back a couple blocks toward where he stood on 4th and J Streets

The next thing O'Connor knew guns were popping all around him. He first saw the Mayor and Sheriff leading the posse on horseback coming after the squatters, then the Mayor was wounded and one of the squatters fell.

Maloney's horse fell and picking himself up, he limped past O'Connor into an alley chased by several deputies. He saw another posse man fall just as a bullet ripped through his own chest and knocked him to the ground. The shooting continued with panic and chaos in the streets without regard for the fallen man.

O'Connor gasped for breath, his hands pressed his right breast as blood seeped through his fingers. He blinked in disbelief as he desperately tried to stay conscious. He saw the priest kneel over him and put pressure on his wound.

"Father," he cried, "is it bad?" But he knew it was.

The priest whispered in his ear, "I'm giving you the

last rites. Is there anything else you'd like to confess?"

Michael's voice was weak, but he pulled the priest close to his mouth and whispered, "Take the money and gold on me and split it between the church and the squatters, will you Father?" Before the priest could respond Michael sputtered, "I have a large cache of gold hidden in a twisted tree by the American river 'bout halfway to Folsom. Dear God!"

He coughed blood, looked the priest in the eyes and took his last breath. After a few moments Father Anderson, eyes closed in prayer, tears flowing down his face, freed his right wrist from Michael's death grip. He cradled Michael's head with one hand and pulled shut his eyelids with the other. He finished the last rites, anointing Michael's forehead, mouth and chest with oil.

Father Anderson eventually confided in his inner circle of church laymen about Michael O'Connor's dying words and the thousand dollars he left to the church and squatters. These men searched in vain, but the story of the gold in the bent tree by the river became a local legend passed down through generations.

The Historic Record

In the battle dubbed "The Squatters' Riot" by the press, Mayor Harlan Bigelow was seriously wounded and City Assessor J. W. Woodland was killed. Charles Robinson was also wounded while Joseph Maloney and squatter Jesse Morgan were killed. History also recalls that two innocent bystanders were killed in the crossfire.

The next day Sheriff McKinney led twenty men to attack a squatters' camp at Brighton, just west across the Sacramento River. The Sheriff and three squatters were killed. It was reported that in the days that followed, the squatters' ranks swelled to hundreds of men who marched at will through the city and threatened to burn it down. Two days later James McClatchy and Richard Moran were released from La Grange (river boat jail). McClatchy went on to found the Sacramento Bee Newspaper. The military was quickly called in from San Francisco to keep the peace and by September 1850 California had become the 31st state in record time.

Part One

Loss lives deep in his chest

Pit bull jaw rattlesnake fangs

clutch at his heart

He wants release

bloody ventricles

to rip apart

but the beast

gnaws and

sucks

CHAPTER ONE - SNAKE PIT

Wednesday, April 10, 2002

J ake the Snake took another swig from the pint of cheap whiskey. The dirty brown glass felt cool on his chapped lips, but his guts clenched at the approaching burn. His grass green eyes sparked through the haze of weed and whiskey and a shock of light brown hair hung down from his Giants baseball cap. He passed the bottle to Mota and, with a shiver, felt the warm numbness calm the beast inside. Mota, a Latino with piercing black eyes and long curly hair, was quick to smile and quicker to grab the bottle.

"Breakfast of Champions!" Mota belched and Snake chuckled.

Snake gulped the last swill and yelled, "Fuck tomorrow!"

"Fuck tomorrow!" echoed Mota.

Snake mocked, "God, why have you forsaken us?

Homeless squatters with nothing but grief and dirt. Hell the dirt ain't even ours, though it's supposed to be a public park."

As expected, Mota's eyes burned like lumps of coal and looked sternly into Snake's eyes.

He spit, "Pendejo! You know I don't like to dis the big guy, we got enough trouble as it is homey."

Being homeless and camping in the riparian forest of the American River Parkway was trouble all right. Between the Sacramento City Police and the County Park Rangers people were constantly being moved along and threatened with citation or arrest. Many of the campers themselves were mentally ill, drug and alcohol addicted or both and if they wanted help or housing there were long waiting lists and rules, *like no dogs or couples allowed* or *you must be sober first*. Then there were the parasites—drug dealers, land speculators, payday loan rip-offs and liquor stores. It wasn't the idyllic, carefree hobo lifestyle that some people claimed.

Sacramento, like any American city, had its titles: The capitol of California, River City, the City of Trees, and land of gold—as well as a soft, putrid underbelly of poverty, racism, addiction and greed. The capitol building,

City Hall, and other halls of power were the true gold mines of today if you had the money and connections to influence political decisions and land development. In California, trillions of dollars were made through the development and sales of housing, while tens of thousands went homeless. Sacramento was a government town with a high percentage of public employees and by most measures Sacramentans were generous and community minded. Local politics leaned to the left.

Campers on the north side of the river had already begun their daily pilgrimage to the St. Francis Village of hospitality and services (called "the Village" or "da vil" by most folks) to get a cup of coffee and day old bread at Dignity Park. Later on the free lunch cooked by community volunteers served hundreds of hungry people every day. Campers trudged with black plastic garbage bags stuffed with their few possessions or rode their bikes over the American River to the old produce warehouses and red brick industrial buildings just north of downtown, where the American and Sacramento Rivers met.

Snake and Mota, campmates in their late thirties, sat in a stand of tall cottonwood trees between the bike trail and the river, but traffic hummed from the nearby

Garden Highway. They were approached by two men on bikes, a large blonde Chou dog with a huge head running behind them.

"Hey Bandana," yelled Snake when he saw them.

"Hey Snake," returned the lead bike guy in a rasping voice, his signature bandana tied around his forehead.

"Hey Gremlin," greeted Mota and the thin one with long, wiry red hair nodded back without saying anything. His dog Jaws approached Mota, who stroked his head and ears. Jaws was legendary for chewing through the metal cages in the Village dog kennel.

Snake extended a new bottle. Bandana took a swig and passed it back, grinning.

Gremlin didn't drink and didn't talk much, so Bandana jumped in, "Gremlin needs some help with the kennel at the Village. They kicked Jaws out 'cause they want him to get fixed, but Gremlin won't and now Jaws ain't welcome in the Village."

Snake and Mota were seen as middle men among the campers in the parkway. They maintained good relations with the Village staff and the police and park rangers, so campers would come to them with all types of requests and they helped when they could.

Mota said, "Why don't you just get him fixed, Gremlin? That's been a rule at the kennel for years now! They'll do it for free at the animal clinic."

Gremlin set his jaw and shook his head "Ah ain't gettin' 'im fixed. Never!" Gremlin was known for his uncompromising attitude, which continually got him in trouble with the police and other authorities. He had been a foster kid and run away. He had little education and much difficulty understanding rules and cues. Snake and Mota knew he wasn't the sharpest knife in the drawer.

"We'll talk to Sam at the Village and see if we can work anything out, but sometimes rules is rules Gremlin," Snake offered.

Bandana rasped, "Thanks guys," and handed Snake a beer as they rode off.

Snake watched slanting sun rays blink through leaves overhead and smelled loamy dirt, green grass and the wide snowmelt river. He was smiling, enjoying his buzz when he was jolted from his reverie by a shrill but familiar scream, which made the hair on his neck stand up. It seemed to come from a thickly wooded depression known as the snake pit. The scream turned into sobbing shrieks as Snake and Mota jumped up and ran unsteadily toward the disturbance.

Snake said, "Sounds like Cat."

Mota yelled, "See, I told you not to fuck with El Señor."

As they entered the snake pit they saw Cat on her knees bending over the feet of two bloodied campers.

"They're dead, they're dead!" Cat wailed.

Mota saw the top of the camouflage bedrolls soaked in blood and yelled, "Shit! It's Tinker & Charlie." Snake and Mota ducked under the brown tarp hung over the camp to check pulses.

Mota cussed. "Damn! Tinker's gone. Looks like gun shots in the back of his head." Snake reached for Charlie's neck and saw that he'd been shot in the face.

He yelled, "He's alive, quick staunch his wound, you're the medic. I'll find someone with a phone." Snake took off to a nearby camp while Mota ripped off a piece of his shirt for Charlie's battered and bleeding face.

A police car with two cops arrived within minutes. They were well known to campers as Batman & Robin. The campers respected them for being fair and helping when they could. A small crowd had arrived, so the dynamic duo had their arms spread wide on either side of the victims yelling, "This is a crime scene, please move back." They asked Cat to stand by so they could question her while Snake and Mota continued to apply first aid.

Snake said, "You guys got here fast. We think Paul is gone, but Charlie's alive and seems to be breathing OK."

Batman checked Paul, Tinker's real name, for a pulse, but found none. He shook his head at the camper's wounds, glancing at his partner who was next to Mota checking Charlie's wound.

"He's unconscious and he's lost a lot of blood," Mota said, looking up at Robin.

The firehouse ambulance arrived a minute later. It bumped down the dirt trail and skid to a stop, a cloud of dust overtaking the vehicle like a specter. Two paramedics checked the victims, pronounced Paul dead, treated Charlie and placed him on a gurney.

Snake, Mota and Cat were given wipes to clean the blood off their hands and then Charlie was whisked away in a cloud of dust. Snake sobbed, shaking badly. Mota's arms were wrapped around the sobbing Cat who clutched him tightly. Snake put his arms around his two friends. Together they watched the ambulance continue to the bike trail. Mota's tears streaked his face and he shook his head staring at Paul's dead body still in his bloody sleeping bag.

"Jesus Christ!" said Mota as he made the sign of the cross.

More police officers arrived to string yellow tape around the site. They were followed by the forensic team which carefully examined the body and combed the area. The homicide detective questioned Snake, Mota and Cat at length and asked the two men if they could accompany the investigators to talk with campers in the area.

Snake spoke in low tones to Mota as they stood aside waiting to take the cops to the adjoining camps.

"How could this happen? Why randomly target two guys who had nothing? This shit doesn't add up."

Mota just shook his head and said, "I've seen my share of dead bodies in Kuwait, but shooting two harmless guys in their sleep? That's just evil!"

Batman and Robin knew many of the campers. Batman briefed the murder investigators. "Paul, the dead man, was deaf and his speech was impaired. He was well-liked by campers who nicknamed him 'the tinker' because he pulled around a metal cart full of tools and parts he'd scrounged. He would fix other people's bikes or carts or whatever they needed. I don't see the cart so it might be at the Village. We can go over to take a look later."

Robin pitched in, "He was a Caucasian in his late forties who was homeless and living on government disability for at least the last five years that we know of. You could usually tell when Paul was around. His voice could be real loud and he would make weird moans and shrieks, but could talk a little. He often drank or smoked weed, but he wasn't into the serious stuff. Compared to some of the hard asses we see out here, these guys were just goofy drunks."

Snake and Mota led the team of detectives through the camps to ask if anyone had seen or heard anything. The snake pit campers were hardcore alcoholics and most were already buzzed in the morning. Pit bull and Lizard, two grizzled Vietnam veterans and friends of the two victims, said they thought they had heard two or three shots in the middle of the night.

Word on the street spread quickly through the camps and the mood among people at the Village was dark and angry. There was talk of revenge and what they'd do to the shooter if they found him. Most campers wouldn't admit to fear, but the seemingly random shooting of folks they knew to be harmless added a new level of worry.

Village staff and guests (staff referred to the hungry and homeless people who used the Village's many services as "guests") were gathered around Paul's cart talking about him and sending prayers to Charlie. Snake, Mota and Cat spent the day retelling their story over and over to Village staff and scores of fellow campers.

Batman and Robin—whose real names were Officers Pat and Rob—spent a lot of time at the Village. They came by later in the day to meet with the director Sam White. Sam had included staff leaders Reverend Don Hood and Sister Julie Baldwin who knew and worked closely with the officers.

Pat and Rob emphasized that their department was serious about finding the shooter, though there wasn't much to go on yet. They were willing to share some information, but asked that nothing leave the room.

Pat started, "The murder squad has taken some casts of boot prints found near the scene, but there were so many footprints that it is tough to say whether we've gotten anything useful."

Rob chimed in. "The coroner estimates time of death

between three and four in the morning. Mercifully, Paul was likely asleep and died from his wounds instantly. We need you to keep your ears open for anything that could be a motive."

Don responded, "Our guests who know them and camped nearby seem just as shocked as we are. So far no one has mentioned anything that makes sense of this."

Sam asked about Charlie and they reported he was stable but they had not been able to talk with him. Rob added, "He's at Sutter Hospital and we might want one of you to meet with him first when he is able, so we don't frighten him." Sam thanked the two officers.

Pat wrapped up the meeting. "Captain Ortega with the homicide squad is in charge of this now; here is his card if you hear anything at all you think might be useful."

That night Cat scored a little smack and since she had a fear of needles, she snorted it all. She holed up in an alley on the north edge of downtown. Her thoughts raced back to Paul. He had been nice to her. Now he was dead. Sure he had made a pass or two, but he was old enough to be her father, so they had both laughed it off. They had often camped in the same area and she had felt safe with Tinker and Charlie nearby.

Tonight she camped away from the river. The alley smelled of piss and rotten food, but she was well hidden behind a dumpster on top of a wooden pallet and under some cardboard. When she finally fell asleep, she dreamed.

She awoke to the sound of footsteps and peered over the top of her sleeping bag to see a tall figure in a long trench coat and wide brimmed hat walking slowly along the trail between camps. His head swiveled left and right. Was he looking for someone? Maybe her?

He kept his hands in his pockets and his hat pulled low. His face was in shadow. Something about him looked familiar, but she couldn't place him. He walked toward her. She closed her eyes and thought, Shit, there's nobody close by. I hope this is a dream. Her right hand felt around and found the knife she kept under the coat she used for a pillow, but the man passed her by.

She watched as he faded into the bush and just as she slipped back into sleep she was startled by three muffled pops.

Her heart pounded against her ribcage as she gasped

awake. Cat was pretty sure that the dream was a memory. She had been camped under a simple tarp tied between trees about a hundred yards from Paul and Charlie the night before.

Snake and Mota hosted a gathering of camping neighbors who were friends of Tinker and Charlie. Pit bull, Lizard, Bandana, Gremlin and two women named China and Jube were sitting in a circle around a lantern. Paranoia was running high, so they had organized a night watch in the area around the shooting. People from neighboring camps came by to offer their condolences as bottles and joints were passed around. Gremlin just kept shaking his head as they told stories about Paul and Charlie.

Bandana in his rasping voice recalled one of the many times Tinker had fixed his bike with some duct tape and wire.

Lizard stammered, "T-T-Tinker always sh-shared his b-b-booze and t-t-tools."

"Hey, has anyone seen Cat?" asked China.

"Snake and I were with her most of the day, but when the park closed she headed downtown. I haven't seen her since," Mota said with a faraway look on his face.

The other campers eventually drifted off and Snake had taken a late shift on the watch. After finishing a half pint of cheap whisky he was now in the tent he shared with Mota. They were both asleep in their bedrolls. Snake dreamed fitfully.

He floated on water and the gentle sway was relaxing. His eyes were closed and the sun warmed his body. God, he loved to float in his pool. His work and financial worries began to melt away.

He suddenly felt himself falling, falling through space. He came to a sudden stop and hovered above his pool. Below him there was a body on the shallow bottom and he squinted to see into the water through the bright sun rays strobing off the surface.

Blood clouded the water. It flowed from two wounds in the back of a man's head—Paul's head. Snake's heart ached. Helplessness overwhelmed him. He watched the body begin to float toward the surface. He reached his bloody hands toward the water to turn the body over, but instead of the face of his friend Paul he was horrified to see the pale and lifeless face of his three-year old daughter Angie. He tried to breathe life into her, but she was gone.

"*Noooooo!*"

Snake awoke to find Mota watching him from his bedroll, shaking his head. Snake was covered in sweat and felt his body shudder.

Mota whispered, "That sounded like a real bad one bro, are you OK?"

Snake looked confused and his head still pounded from the whiskey and the dream. "I've got to get some help before I fucking lose it. Finding Paul and Charlie really tweaked my head."

Chapter Two - It Takes a Village

Thursday, April 11, 2002

Sam White, forty-seven year old director of St. Francis Village, sat in his office the morning after the murder. Sam was over six feet tall with long arms, broad shoulders and big hands. His jeans and short sleeved denim shirt matched the blues in his eyes. His fingers combed through longish sandy hair then smoothed a bushy mustache and goatee that were both turning white.

Sam was a clinical social worker with a long career in mental health and homeless programs. He was a founder of the Sacramento Homeless Organizing Committee (SHOC) and several other advocacy groups.

Sam picked up the *Sacramento Bee*, his reading glasses balanced halfway down his large, slightly crooked nose. The story of the murder was on the front page of the Metro section.

Homeless Men Shot in American River Parkway

(April 11, 2002) by Monica Fuentes

"Sacramento police are investigating the
deaths of two homeless men found shot to death
in their camp early Wednesday morning. Paul
Dixon, a forty-six year old "camper," appeared to
have died of gunshot wounds to the head. Paramedics pronounced him dead at the scene. The
other victim, a middle-aged Caucasian man, was
taken to the hospital for head wounds. Police are
withholding his identity at this time. Police have
yet to determine a motive or suspect in this case.
Police Captain Michael Ortega is asking anyone
with information to contact the department at the
number listed below."

It seemed that the police hadn't discovered much yet.
Sam knew it had only been a day, but he worried that this
case would be swept under the rug with so many of the
other dangers facing the homeless. The campers in the
Village were already in a dark mood with the shooting of
Paul and Charlie hanging over them.

Sam turned to the next page. He skimmed the other stories briefly before an article titled "The Homeless Problem" caught his eye. He remembered that reporter. They had interviewed him about the campers in the Village.

It was largely what he expected. The article started by bemoaning the high number of homeless men and women in Sacramento. It went on to talk about some of the struggles faced by the Village campers. Dick Regina, a County Supervisor went on about how the County was already doing enough for homeless people and they needed to beef up enforcement of the anti-camping law. Sam and his ally City Councilman Kalen Jones were quoted and both spoke of the vulnerability of homeless people sleeping outside and the need for more housing and shelter.

Unfortunately the article also quoted Bill Buckmeister, commercial property owner and business association leader who blamed the murder "on the lawlessness of the illegal campers in the river parkway who also defile the habitat along the river. The city needs a tougher policy to root these trolls out of the parkway to make it safe for legitimate users."

Sam blurted out loud, "Jesus! Really Buck? Trolls? What an asshole!" He was used to Buck's bullshit, but this was below the belt. He looked at the front Metro page photo of Dignity Park guests hovering around Paul's cart and tears welled up. A Bee columnist had also quoted Buck and ranted about how homeless people were destroying the river parkway and that the Village was a magnet for deplorable junkies and winos. *The usual victim blaming, as if the treatment of people with addictions and mental illness had nothing to do with the rest of us.*

The violent killing of this gentle disabled man, his own age, really hurt and angered him. His commitment to this work was motivated by love and service, but he had learned that his anger at injustice was what drove him on through burn-out and grief. A psychiatrist he worked with as a young social worker had told him that anger and hate were just frustrated love. *So it always comes back around to love*, he reminded himself. He tried to focus on preparing for today's monthly Board of Director's meeting, checking written reports and financial statements.

He supervised over a dozen program directors who managed Dignity Park, Dorothy Day House (Women's

Crisis Center), the Dining Room, HomeSchool and several other programs at the Village. The program directors in turn supervised a staff of about sixty total employees, which included over twenty part-time homeless and also hundreds of volunteers. Sam was responsible for raising over two million dollars each year and the Village didn't seek or accept government funding. It was a constant struggle, but made easier by thousands of loyal financial supporters.

Three hours later Sam sat at the head of a large conference table chairing the Board of Directors meeting. He filled them in on what little he knew about the murder investigation. There was a discussion about Paul's memorial service and it was agreed that the Village would pay to bring his family to the service if necessary. Paul's death and the onslaught of homeless bashing had hit everyone hard and their anger fueled action.

Sister Julie updated the Board on the increasing numbers of women and children being turned away from shelters since the closure of the temporary winter shelters at the end of March.

"We have between thirty and fifty women and kids at Day House at the end of each day with nowhere to go for shelter," she said. "We're handing out blankets and wishing them good luck."

Don Hood, the director of Dignity Park who had ridden with the freedom riders in the South during the civil rights movement, raised his voice to preaching level. "This is unacceptable and if more people in our community knew that scores of women and children are being abandoned to the streets on a nightly basis they'd be outraged. We need a sit-in or other direct action to raise public awareness. The county is responsible for welfare programs, so we could target their offices."

The Board was ready for action and everyone chimed in, "Let's do something to honor Paul's memory."

Sister Julie said, "We need more housing and shelter beds, but all we hear about is cracking down on campers." Heads nodded in agreement and then Sister Julie made the motion that the Village lead a non-violent sit-in in the lobby of the County Board of Supervisors offices during business hours until their demands were met. The Board unanimously voted in favor. Don volunteered to start a calendar of volunteer shifts for the sit-in.

Sam noted, "We have to work through our specific demands, numbers of housing and shelter units, so it's clear what we want and we have to be committed to sticking with this long term."

—————————

Soon after the Board meeting Jake Winters (Snake), Moreno Fierro (Mota) and Oretha Johnson (Cat) sat in Sam White's office looking frazzled and hung over. Cat explained the dream she'd had and the vague description of the murderer.

"Glad you came in Oretha," said Sam who tried to use camper's real names if he knew them.

Snake said, "Shit, Cat, you should talk to the police and let them decide if it's helpful or not."

But she was shaking her head. "I got a no-show warrant and I don't wanna go to jail."

Sam agreed with Jake that her description might be important to the investigation.

"Let me call Batman and Robin," he suggested, "and see if they will agree not to arrest you since you're coming forward voluntarily. I'll see if they can meet with us later." Cat nodded her assent.

An hour later they were gathered in Sam's office. Batman explained to Cat that they would overlook the warrant if she promised to attend the next day's legal clinic at the Village so she could schedule a court date for her camping ticket. With this agreement, Cat felt safe enough to come forward openly. She told the officers about her dream—and how she felt sure that it was a memory.

The officers listened to her story patiently and said it was important she came forward because her description corroborated another campers' description of someone they saw in the area acting strange the night of the murder.

Robin said, "Your memory of the murderer looking for someone makes the shooting seem less random than we originally thought."

Sam thanked everyone and said, "I hope this crime can be resolved quickly, the campers are really on edge."

The officers nodded and Batman said, "We don't have a whole lot to go on yet, but we promise you we are taking this very seriously."

After the dynamic duo left, Snake shot a guilty glance at Mota. He asked Sam, "Do you have a few minutes to talk about a personal matter?"

Sam said, "Sure." He was thinking of all the phone calls he still needed to make, but if one of the campers needed his help he would gladly offer it. Then Sam hugged Oretha and Moreno goodbye, saying, "I know this has hit us all like a ton of bricks, especially you three who found them, but let's keep poking around. Let me know what you hear on the streets. Take care of yourselves."

Sam had known Jake for over a year and really liked him. Despite his heavy drinking, Jake had stepped up as a leader among homeless campers and wasn't afraid to testify at City Council meetings or speak with the media. Jake was smart and compassionate with a sense of humor, but had a self-destructive streak that Sam recognized as the deep trauma, guilt and grief that many homeless folks carried around. Sam had heard some rumors, something about Jake's young daughter dying, but Jake had never spoken to him about it.

Sam closed his door and sat down.

"I've never told you my story, but I need to talk to someone. In fact I haven't talked much about it since I first told the police what happened," Jake explained, his voice tightening. Sam encouraged Jake by nodding and leaning forward to listen.

"I was married with two kids—living the dream in our small home with a pool and a decent job, but I lost it all like that," Jake said, snapping his fingers. "I was home one Saturday, my wife was out running errands with our six year old son and I had our three year old daughter Angie." Saying her name choked him up and tears started to run down his cheeks.

"I'm sorry to lay this on you man, but after seeing Paul's dead body I've been having nightmares and crying for no reason. I feel like I'm losing it."

"I'm glad you're willing to tell me this," Sam said gently. "I know it hurts, but telling your story is the first step towards healing."

Jake swallowed hard a couple times and continued, "Angie and I had been swimming, then we came inside and she got into one of her kid TV shows. I thought I'd just head down to the basement and smoke a little weed and pump some weights. I was only down there for like ten minutes. When I came back upstairs the TV was still on, but I didn't see her, so I called for her.

"She didn't answer. Our house wasn't that big, so she should have heard me even if she was out back. I started to worry and then I ran out to the pool and saw her floating face down in the water." His voice tightened again and the tears were flowing in earnest. He barely choked out the next sentence. "I jumped in, turned her over and tried to breathe life into her, but she was gone."

Sam came around the desk to put a hand on Jake's shoulder. "My God Jake, how awful! I can't imagine what losing my daughter would feel like."

"I still can't believe it—sometimes I feel like I'm going to wake up and see her beautiful face smiling at me, watching me as I sleep in the morning. I still don't know how she got into the pool so fast, the gate was closed, but I'd left a chair close to the fencing around the pool and she climbed like a little monkey. We always made her wear her floaties to swim, but she didn't have them on." He shuddered and started sobbing. Sam let him cry in silence for a minute, hand still on his shoulder. Sam offered tissues and Jake wiped his face.

"I was lucky they didn't charge me with child endangerment, but I never told them I was downstairs getting high. In fact you and my wife and Mota are the only ones I've ever told. I just fell apart after that, I started drinking heavy. My wife said she didn't blame me, but it was never the same between us. I should have been there for her. She tried to hang in with me for about six months but I was so guilty and depressed I didn't want to do anything but drink. I lost my job when I came to work drunk one too many times. Right after that I got a DUI. My wife told me in jail, 'maybe it would be better if you don't come home. At least not until you stop drinking.' "I was too ashamed to face my family anyway, so I just hit the streets."

"Jake, I can't know how losing your daughter feels, but let's face it, you are the parent and responsible adult. You've got to make amends to your family and find some forgiveness for yourself. You still have a family that needs you, but you have to get straight first. I've told you before that you're a natural leader and are looked up to by a lot of campers who are crushed by their own losses. You have a lot to give to others and a lot to live for, especially your son." Sam hesitated for a moment. "If you're ready to put down the bottle I can get you some help."

After a pause, Jake whispered, "I think I'm ready."

Sam quickly responded "Okay, I'll call Tony at 'Living Sober' and they'll get you started right now, but it won't be easy. What about Moreno? I know he's your good friend, but you guys may need to part ways. You'll need to be around other people who aren't drinking. I'll talk to Moreno and make him the same offer I'm making you.

Does he know you want to quit?"

"Yeah, he knows I'm thinking about it, but he didn't say anything about wanting to join me." Jake's look of desperation softened and a ray of hope lit his face. "I'm so tired of the life and I think I'm ready, thanks Sam."

"You're the one who had the courage to share your story and to seek help bro, that's a good first step. I'll call Tony and walk you over to Living Sober to make sure you get connected."

After the warm hug that always came with seeing Tony Ruiz at Living Sober, Sam looked at Tony and nodded towards Jake. Tony knew Jake and, smiling, said, "Are you ready Jake?"

Jake began to fidget and look down. "You know finding Paul freaked me out. I find myself crying for no reason and having nightmares. I thought I was ready, but I'm not sure." Jake's thoughts turned to whiskey and his overwhelming need to numb the pain he felt. "Give me until the end of the day, OK?"

Tony said, "If you leave now Jake, you won't be back today. I'll take you into the AA meeting in half an hour and I'll try to find you a space at our 'New Life' recovery home for tonight. It won't be easy, but you'll have the support you'll need when you commit to sobriety. Tell me the truth Jake. You're already thinking about getting a bottle, aren't you?"

"Yeah I'm thinking about it, but I think I can hold off. Look, I just have to tie up some loose ends and take care of some business. Thanks Tony, but I need to think about it."

Sam chimed in, "You should take Tony up on his offer Jake, there's nothing more important than getting sober and getting your life back." Privately Sam knew that Jake wouldn't be back if he left now, but he said, "I hope you'll come back later Jake," and shook the camper's hand.

On the way back to his office Sam saw Mota and Cat riding their bikes at the end of the street, pedaling away from the Village. Mota had probably seen Jake go into Tony's office and he reminded himself to put the word out that he wanted to talk with Mota. He checked his cell phone and saw that his wife Sheila Bright had called, as had council member Kalen Jones.

He walked upstairs to his office. First he called Sheila at work. She was the Director of the Care for All Health Clinic in Midtown.

"Hi sweetie I just saw you called. It's been crazy here as usual, everyone's freaked about the shooting."

"I'm sorry to hear that, but not surprised. I just called to remind you of our fundraiser tomorrow night at Luna's Cantina at six."

"Yeah I remembered, I'm looking forward to a TGIF margarita and tacos. How did ticket sales go?"

"We're almost sold out, so let your staff know there's only a few tickets left. I love you and I'll see you later."

"Love you too. See you later."

Council member Jones was a 40 year old former professional football player for the San Francisco Forty-Niners and community activist who grew up in the Heights and had come back to Sacramento after his sports career. They'd become friends as community organizers of progressive causes over the years and Sam was one of his key supporters.

Sam called Kalen on his cell phone and he answered on the first ring. "Hey Sam, I'm in a meeting, but I wanted to let you know I asked Carly to help you with your media response. Are you going to be at Luna's tomorrow night?"

"Of course, I'll see you there and we can talk. Thanks

for sending in the cavalry, you think it's that bad, eh?"

"Yeah, it's bad, we'll talk."

Right after he hung up he got a call from Monica Fuentes, the *Bee* Metro reporter. He had given her many story leads and quotes over the years. She was a competent and sympathetic reporter.

"Hi Sam, how are you holding up?"

"I'm hanging in there. I thought you did a nice job on the story."

"Thanks, anything new on the case? Have you heard how the surviving victim is doing?"

"I hear he's stable, but can't or doesn't want to talk to anyone. I can only imagine he's pretty freaked out."

Before she said goodbye, Monica gave Sam a heads-up that she'd gotten some pretty controversial quotes from "Buck" on a follow-up story about the business district and that they'd probably be in tomorrow's paper.

Bill Buckmeister, a multi-millionaire landowner, could always be counted on to call homeless people "bums and criminals" and the agencies that serve them, particularly St. Frances Village, "Magnets and Enablers." Fortunately many of the big downtown developers and landowners thought Buckmeister an embarrassment.

They had learned that street outreach and service programs for homeless folks also helped the business environment and that if folks were ablebodied they wanted to work, but Buck seemed to be the voice of a small segment of the population.

As he was packing his bag to leave the Village, Sam's phone rang. "Hi, this is Sam."

"Hi Sam, it's Carly." Carly Johnson was Kalen's sometime girlfriend and long-time political advisor. She was an attorney, an extraordinary fundraiser, and local political power broker.

"Thanks for calling Carly, Kalen gave me a heads up."

"The short version is that you have to go on the offensive Sam. Buck has jumped on the killing and has been very busy calling and meeting with key people." Carly quickly laid out a plan that involved meeting with the local newspaper editors, City Council, County Supervisors and key staff all in the next two weeks, which only she with Kalen's help could pull off.

Sam added, "Our Board of Directors met today and agreed we should go on the offensive. In honor of Paul, the guy who was shot, we are planning a sit-in at the County building for early next week. We hope to shift the focus to women and children and push the county for more housing and shelter."

"Wow a sit-in, that's different. It might cause some backlash in the short term," Carly warned. Sam agreed with her and they set a meeting time for the next morning at ten to go over their demands. Carly added, "We might have a meeting as soon as tomorrow with supervisor Regina who is an important swing vote at the county."

"Yeah, I saw what he said in the paper and it didn't bode well. Thanks Carly, see you tomorrow."

Chapter Three - Fun and Games in Bum's World

Friday, April 12, 2002

Sam and Sheila sat back on their Adirondack chairs facing into the rising sun from the deck in their back yard. Their coffees steamed in mugs. Sheila made notes on her calendar and thought about everything she had to do, which included making sure all the pieces of her fundraiser came together that evening. Sam was rubbing the rabbit-soft ears of their chocolate lab Kabu. She sat at attention, her broad chest and silky reddish brown coat fire-lit by a beam of sun, head cocked to one side. A crooked smile showed she enjoyed the attention.

"Hey Bu girl!" said Sam, smiling.

Between bites of bagel, Sam asked Sheila if he could help with anything for the fundraiser, but she shook her head no.

"From everything you told me last night—the civil

disobedience action, the fallout from the murder, the meetings with the elected and media—you've got your hands full."

"Carly's trying to set up a meeting with Regina today to see where he will stand on our housing and shelter demands. He's the swing vote. You'd think he'd be with us as a Democrat. But he seems to be positioning as more of a conservative. I think he plans to run for the Assembly next year. Anyway, I'm on call for Carly all day if she can set up meetings."

Sheila reminded Sam that she was going to Oakland Saturday to spend the night with her half-sister and went inside to get ready for work. Because, Sam and Sheila didn't have children, their mornings were taken at their own pace. He had been thirty-two and she thirty-seven when they became a couple. They had met as peace activists in the early eighties, trying to keep the Reagan Administration from attacking Central America. Sam had helped raise Sheila's younger half-sisters when their mother was killed by a drunk driver in a terrible crash years ago. The girls were out in the world now doing well. They were more like daughters than sisters-in-law to Sam and Sheila was more like a mom than a sister to them.

Sam tossed Kabu a Frisbee and she flew off the deck sprinting ten yards, muscles rippling then jumping to snag it in mid-flight before it crashed into the old apricot tree. Tail wagging vigorously, she bounded up on the deck to return her prize.

Sam said, "Good girl!" then threw her a few more before starting his daily yoga.

A little after eight Sam arrived at the bustling Village. He walked into the women's dining room. The noise of kids and volunteers and the smell of bacon and eggs filled his senses.

He saw Chris, the director of the dining room, and joked, "Is it Cordon Bleu today for seven hundred?" He hugged her and she smiled.

"I hope turkey chili will do, you know we've got the St. Anne's group today and they are trouble." She nudged the shoulder of a gray-haired volunteer in a Village apron stirring a five gallon pot.

The volunteer beamed back at them, then his expression became serious as he said, "So sorry to hear about the shooting."

Sam nodded and the smile slipped off his face. "We're all a bit shook up by it." The volunteer nodded sympathetically, and Sam bid him goodbye. Then he walked to Dorothy Day House to talk to Sister Julie.

Julie Baldwin was sixty years young and had been a Roman Catholic, Sacred Heart Sister for thirty-five of those years. Sam felt her radiate calm as her eyes, one blue and one greenish-gold, smiled at him. Besides running the Crisis Center she often helped Sam with advocacy, representing the Village on community task forces and in the media. She and her staff were fearless in their work with destitute women and mothers.

Homeless women and children, prostitutes, victims of sexual assault and domestic violence, drug addicts and the severely mentally ill came through the Crisis Center every weekday. Julie and her small team tried to find services for their beloved "Guests." When Crisis Center staff couldn't find services, due to long waiting lists or bureaucratic red tape, Sister Julie led the charge. She and her staff were persistent, direct and didn't take "No" for an answer when it came to protecting the vulnerable, but there simply weren't enough shelter beds or other resources.

"Good morning Sister Julie."

"Good morning Sam, how is Charlie doing?"

"He's stable, but has lost an eye and possibly some hearing. I'll try to see him tomorrow."

"Any progress on the murder?"

"Nothing in the last twenty-four hours, which isn't good."

"No, it's not," she agreed.

Sam added, "Don's pulling together Paul's memorial service for Wednesday and we hope his father and step-mom will be here."

"Good, what else is on your mind?"

"Carly's coming by to talk strategy at ten. Can you get away from here for a bit?"

"Sure, I'm excited the Board is really behind this sit-in."

Sam offered, "You know you and your staff are going to have your hands full, dealing with the usual crises, keeping tabs of the numbers of women and kids going without shelter each night and showing up for the sit-in, etc. So I was wanted to offer to fund another staff position, for at least as long as the sit-in lasts. "

Sister Julie nodded. "At the staff meeting this morning everyone got on board, but we could definitely use the help. We're really frustrated so many of the women and children walk back to the streets each night, so we're ready to turn our attention to increasing resources." In the front lobby a woman erupted in anguished cries that turned to deep sobs. Sister Julie glanced at a staffperson who went out to try to comfort her. "Anything else Sam?"

"Carly's trying to set a meeting with Supervisor Regina. He's the swing vote and his comment in the paper was that the county is doing enough on homeless programs and they have more pressing needs like adding Sheriffs and Park Rangers."

Julie shook her head. "Can I join you if you get a meeting with him?"

"Absolutely, I was hoping you'd want to be part of that conversation."

Shaking her head again she was distracted by a woman sitting in a folding chair, a yellow puddle expanding on the beige tiled floor beneath her.

"You want me to send someone over to clean this up?" asked Sam.

"No, we've got it," waved Sister Julie.

"See you soon," said Sam as he headed out the front door and onto A Street.

He squinted into the bright morning sun as he

walked across the busy street through scores of homeless people and past the warehouse, the receiving dock busy with a line of cars waiting to drop off donations.

Sam stopped at the end of A Street where it met the light rail tracks. He came in the front gates of Dignity Park, where several hundred men and a smattering of women were hanging out. They slept on benches, talked to friends or themselves, and found comfort in the shade of the Park's trees and covered outbuildings.

The Park posted simple rules: "No Drugs or Alcohol, No Weapons, No Violence!" Park staff, identified by their green hats, were spaced strategically. They talked to guests, answered questions, and kept watch for any escalating conflict.

Looking left Sam passed "the woodpile," named by the tweaked meth addicts who gathered loosely there. On the other side of the Park was a grassy knoll with shade trees, where people laid sleeping on bedrolls next to a long trailer with several offices. Here guests could store their backpacks or plastic bags, see a nurse, or check for housing programs. Despite the pain and confusion Sam felt in the aftermath of the shooting the Village still needed his attention.

Sam saw Reverend Don, a retired Presbyterian minister and director of the park over by the Memorial Wall. *Paul's name will be up there soon*, he thought as his throat tightened. Don met Sam with his firm handshake and a smile that made his brown eyes twinkle.

Sam stated the obvious: "Looks like you're busy today."

Don nodded. "People are really jumpy after the murder. We had a fight this morning and lots of shouting. Any progress on finding the killer?"

"Not that I know of, it doesn't look good," Sam replied.

Don said, "I've been in touch with Paul's family in Kansas and his father and stepmom are planning to come out here for his memorial service."

"Thanks Don, I'm glad that worked out."

Don added, "I'm excited about our sit-in and proud of the Board for taking it on. It's a great way to honor Tinker and we can change the discussion from more cops in the Parkway to housing solutions."

"Thanks for your leadership on this Don. It looks like Tuesday is on for starting the sit-in. How are you and Sister Julie doing with the faith leaders? I just saw her, but forgot to ask."

"We should have a good turn out to kick things off. Most of the clergy are very supportive and we have about ten confirmed to be there. I think focusing on the women and children should draw people in. But don't forget about all these men we've got with nowhere to go too."

"I know," sighed Sam.

Don nodded and suddenly sped away toward a loud altercation. Sam walked back across the street stopping to shake hands with people he knew, then went upstairs to his office to check messages and to meet with Carly.

Carly was already in his office when he arrived, let in by Ruth, the office manager who was making small talk and pouring a cup of coffee.

"Sorry I'm here early," offered Carly.

"No sweat," replied Sam, smiling at Ruth. "I see you're in good hands."

Ruth backed out of the room, saying, "Just yell if you need more coffee, okay."

Carly pointed at the poster on the back of Sam's door. "I like that."

It read:

SHOW UP

PAY ATTENTION

TELL THE TRUTH WITHOUT BLAME OR
JUDGEMENT

BE OPEN TO OUTCOME

DON'T BE ATTACHED TO OUTCOME

Sam said, "Sheila made me that after reading a book by Angeles Arrien."

Carly jumped in. "I've got us meeting with Supervisor Regina this morning at ten-forty-five, so I wanted to come early to go over our talking points. Is Sister Julie gonna be able to join us?"

Sam nodded. "Sister Julie should be here at ten, so we'll have to go over strategy quickly and head to the meeting. Thanks for setting this up so fast Carly."

"I mentioned your intention to sit-in at the supervisor's offices and he suggested we meet immediately. He's dug in pretty good on this issue and I'm not optimistic. Without his vote we won't get a quick response to your action and positions could harden in the short term."

"I know," said Sam. "We're in this for the long haul and they will get very tired of us after a while."

Sister Julie joined them and after a quick strategy discussion they headed to the County Building. They were soon inside Supervisor Regina's office. His well-known staff person, Danny Aguilar, served them water and coffee while they waited for his boss.

"What's this about a sit-in?" asked Danny.

"Let's wait until Dick is here," said Carly, "I hear you may be moving on to the Assembly?"

"The Supervisor hasn't formally announced yet, but he is considering a run," said Danny.

The door opened and the tall, suited Supervisor walked in and shook hands with his visitors, his smile a bit tight.

"Carly, you asked for this meeting and I've made time for friends, so what can I help you with?"

Carly turned to Sam. "I'm working with Sam on a public response to the murder in the parkway."

Sam took the cue. "Supervisor, we are very disappointed at the political response to this tragedy. Talk of a law enforcement solution to camping is not what we need. We are experiencing significant increases in the number of women, children, and disabled people coming to us for help." He turned to Sister Julie. "Sister Julie, please share with the Supervisor your experience at Day House."

"Supervisor, at Day House alone we see over one hundred homeless women and small children every day. Half of these vulnerable people are sleeping outside or at best, in their cars. We cannot find room for them in shelters or other programs, so we send them off with blankets each night hoping they will be safe on the street. Yes, we have a fund that can house a few families each night, but it's a drop in the bucket. We see our guests returning to violent situations because it's the only place to house their kids. We see sick children who are missing far too much school and disabled women unable to care for themselves.

"We have forty to fifty women and children every day when Day House closes. We need more shelter, housing and support services that families and disabled people can access quickly."

Sister Julie turned back to Sam who said, "The Village Board of Directors has pledged to stage a sit-in in your lobby until the county steps up to adequately deal with this crisis."

The Supervisor gave Sam a stern look and said, "I've told Carly that I think we've done enough for homeless people in this county and now we need to protect regular citizens from the blight of illegal camping and I am supporting more park ranger and police positions to deal with this problem. As far as a sit-in is concerned I'd warn you not to make enemies of your friends with these kinds of threats."

Sam wanted to respond, *with friends like you who needs enemies*, but he bit his tongue and said, "We'll be sharing your position and our demands with the public and our fifteen-thousand supporters. I'd urge you to reconsider and vote with your fellow democratic Supervisors to address real needs. We would rather work together with you, but this enforcement approach will utterly fail at a time when we need more shelter and affordable housing."

"I'll take that under advisement. If you'll excuse me I have some other constituents waiting."

That morning Mota was working on a couple six-packs with Lizard and Pit bull. The random violence had made them jumpy and angry. They were still guarding their camp, pulling all-nighters and drinking heavily. Pit bull's jowly face was a masterpiece of alcoholism and "Don't Fuck with me."

The thin, scaly skinned Lizard stuttered, "M-m-ark m-m-my words. We're g-g-gonna get the s-s-sombitch that shot our friends, ch-chickenshit assholes!"

Pit bull's gravel voice croaked, "Hey, we heard a rumor that Jake got into Living Sober and is staying at their apartments."

"Really? He didn't come back to camp last night, so I wondered if I'd lost my camp partner." Mota was disoriented by Jake's abandonment. He'd stayed away from the Village that day and started drinking early.

Pit bull raised a can of beer, "Here's to our program, it's called Dying Drunk." They all laughed.

Mota joked, "We don't need no twelve steps. We've got three easy steps: open your bottle; drink it; get drunk."

Cat came by after having lunch at the Village and had a beer with them. Batman and Robin cruised over and told them they had to move on.

Cat told Mota, "I know a camp that's selling crystal over on the Island. You got any cash?" Mota was one of the few campers who had Veterans disability income. He'd suffered injuries in the first Desert Storm.

Mota said, "I don't much like meth." But he wanted to

hang out with Cat. "Yeah I got some cash, let's ride."

Cat said, "I don't do it everyday like the woodpile, but when I'm feeling blue sometimes I need a pick-me-up."

They were soon riding their bikes through the canopy of tall cottonwoods and vines. They pedaled up the Garden Highway under the 5 Freeway to the "Island" just north of where the Sacramento and American Rivers met. It was a peninsula most of the time, unless the river swelled.

They cruised along a dirt trail with a smattering of camps and passed a tree house that was cleverly camouflaged. A little farther onto the "island" they came to a camp that was in some trees not far from the bank of the Sacramento River. Radiating out from the tent for about twenty feet was a scattering of bicycle parts and other junk. Mota and Cat recognized the detritus of serious tweakers who stayed up all night talking a mile a minute and tinkering with bicycles and any other crap that was at hand.

Cat whispered, "Jan talks crazy, but she's harmless." Then she called out to the couple Jan and Dave who lived in the camp. A dog growled back and they spotted a black and white pit bull as it stalked out of the large tent and confronted them.

Jan stepped out behind the dog and saw it was Cat who was a semi-regular customer.

"Sit, Lucky!" Jan commanded, and the dog stopped growling and laid down on the ground.

Jan's sunken face had a maniacal smile with a couple teeth like a collapsed jack-o-lantern. She was skin and bones looking much older than her forty years.

She said, "Who's your friend Cat, is it mouse?" Cat introduced Mota, who said he'd met them once before.

Then Jan's partner Dave walked out briskly from the tent and said, "Welcome to Bum's World!"

Both he and Jan looked pretty high, talking rapidly. Jan rambled on, mumbling, "Cops, cops, fucking thieves, secret bullshit, who the fuck? Bond, Bond, James Bond, shoot me please." She ended this tirade with a shrieking laugh.

Dave invited them inside the large tent, which was strewn with trash. Cat sat on a folding chair and Mota's skin crawled as he sat on fouled blankets.

Cat had been here many times before, and asked Dave for "a double." Mota handed Dave a twenty. Dave took out a metal box and opened it. He pulled out two corners of a plastic bag, the white powder secured with rubber bands.

He asked if they were "shootin or snortin" and both Mota and Cat replied "snort." Dave handed them the bags, a straw and a battered little hand mirror. He mixed some powder in a vial with clear liquid and pulled a hypodermic needle from his box for himself and Jan. He inserted the needle into the vial, lifted the plunger and asked Jan if she wanted to go first.

She said, "Sure do, but do me okay." Dave injected half of the meth into a vein on the top of her scabbed, shaking hand. Then Dave took it and did the same thing with the other half to the back of his bruised hand.

Cat and Mota were busy snorting the powder in lines on the mirror and they were both feeling the burn in their nostrils and the rush of the speed. Their breath quickened, sweat beaded on their foreheads and they were soon all talking fast and laughing. Mota offered a joint and they all smoked some weed.

Jan amped up her unintelligible ramble: "Liars, liars, god damned pigs, fucking assholes think they scare me, the fucking president knows, can't do nothin 'bout shit."

Dave said, "Don't mind her, she just goes off when she gets high."

For a while, nobody talked—not to each other, anyway. They rambled to themselves, Jan scratching at her arms the whole time. Cat ignored her and enjoyed the high while it lasted.

Then Dave said, "I heard you two found Tinker & Charlie shot up?" Both Cat and Mota nodded and shivered as they pictured the murder scene. "Have you heard about Charlie telling some campers that Paul had found someone's buried stash?"

Mota shook his head. "It's the first I've heard of that, do you know who Charlie talked to?"

Dave just shook his head thinking, *Yeah I know who he talked to*. But instead he said, "You know what the street telegraph is like, it could be total bullshit."

Something about Dave gave Cat the willies. She looked at Mota and they silently gave the nod that it was time to go. Cat said they needed to get back to their camps, so they said their goodbyes and got on their bikes.

Pedaling away Mota asked, "Did you hear anything about Paul finding a stash?"

"No, you think that's what got Tinker shot?"

"We better ask around."

They stopped to relieve themselves and Mota looked more carefully at the too thin, but athletically built Cat. Her corkscrew curls blew across her face and even though her nose was swollen and her eyes were watering he thought she looked cute. She noticed him watching her and she smiled.

She approached the older Mota, kissed him, and grabbed his butt, and they rolled around in the tall grass together kissing and close. Snake had been like an older brother to her, but she had always thought Mota sexy. She also sensed he was interested, but neither of them had ever made a move. They laid side by side looking up at a beautiful spring sky.

"So you think you've lost your campmate? You guys have been together for awhile."

"Yeah, if the rumors are true. Snake has been a good friend for over a year and I'll miss him. I guess I'm glad he's doing what he needs to do. I know being away from his family is killing him. He has worse dreams than I do and mine are bad."

She prodded, "I heard you saw action in Kuwait and you were in some Chupacabra band. They were kind of famous a few years back, weren't they?"

"Yeah, I served in a MASH unit in Kuwait. Saw more blood than I was prepared for, mostly the other side and civilians, but we put our share of GIs back together too. It fucked me up. I got bombed riding a truck and I got a head injury. I still have nightmares and weird flashbacks.

"After the service I started playing music with old friends and the coke flowed. I met my wife when the band got started, she was younger and a partier. We had it goin' on for about three years, making decent money at gigs here and the Bay Area, but then it went to shit and we broke up."

"What about your family?"

"I got a brother in San Fransisco, but he's all the family I got left. My ex is in Stockton and we talk some-times. She cheated on me with my so-called friend the drummer and they got hitched. It was my fault too. I was always partying and fucking around on her. It caught up to us. Thank God we didn't have kids."

"What about your family?"

"I got brothers and sisters that live in the Heights, but my folks are dead. We don't talk much. Lost a baby girl to CPS when I was eighteen - my family didn't want her, so she went up for adoption. I got really depressed, like suicidal, you know? The baby was fine. I wasn't using that much and I was snorting the good stuff. I didn't have no crack baby!"

Holding up his hands he said, "I feel you babe. I don't throw no stones, my house is cracked glass."

"Hey you're alone now and I'm freaked out about camping by myself. You think we could camp together tonight?" she asked.

"Well, let's go to my camp and see if Jake is really gone. I mean you're welcome to camp with us either way. Its been awhile since I was with someone if you know what I mean." They kissed again and she said, "I do know what you mean."

He slowly rose up, crouched into a shooting stance and made a gun out of his right hand. He swiveled his hips, sweeping the gun around towards Cat, and imitated Jan: "Bond, Bond, James Bond."

Cat cracked up repeating, "Bond, Bond, James Bond, shoot me please." Laughing, they repeated some of her other crazy ramblings as they pedaled out of the Parkway to the nearest gas station and bought a six pack.

Just after sunset they got to the large camouflage

tarp nestled into a thick stand of cottonwood and honey locust trees that Mota had shared with Snake.

It looked like Snake had taken his few clothes and toiletries and had just left his bedroll and other camp stuff. There was no note and part of him still wondered if Snake had really joined Living Sober. Now he saw that Snake really *had* gone—and he was alone.

Buzzing along on the speed they drank beers and smoked joints with camping neighbors Lizard and Pit bull, commiserating about the absence of Snake who had been a leader in the camp.

"Hey Cat," growled Pit bull, "you want to join our new program? It's called Dying Drunk."

"Sure, you know I am highly qualified," Cat shot back and Pit bull laughed deeply until he started coughing.

Later their other neighbors and Cat's friends China and Jube stopped by. These two women were a couple and had recently gotten clean from meth addictions, going cold turkey. They both had part time jobs at the Village now.

China and Jube were as different as night and day. Jube was black like ebony with a wide muscular body, a large smile and a short afro. China - who was part

Philipino and thus inappropriately nicknamed - was tiny with pale skin and long black hair streaked with pink and blue.

Mota asked them if Charlie had talked to anyone about Paul finding someone's stash before he was shot. They hadn't heard the rumor, so Mota asked them to discretely poke around.

When they were alone he told Cat, "I might try to talk to Charlie at the hospital in the morning if I can get in."

Cat said, "I've got to work at da vil in the morning, but I could meet you over at the hospital later."

"I didn't know you had a job."

"I only work Saturday mornings, but its a foot in the door."

"Good for you. We better try to crash. I don't know about you, but meth hangovers fuck me up."

"Yeah, I have to be careful, I've been partying heavy since the shooting. I don't want to be stuck in the wood-pile."

Cat pulled her duffle from the back of her bike, took out her sleeping bag and laid it out next to Mota's. They made themselves comfortable.

They looked intensely at each other and then kissed hard and long. *This chick is hot,* thought Mota as he yanked his long-sleeved T-shirt off. Snake's motto came to mind.

"Fuck tomorrow!" he yelled.

Cat yelled it back and they laughed together. She took off her sweater and blouse in one quick move. They kissed again, her breasts pressing against his chest. Soon they were naked in Mota's bedroll, bodies warm and wet. They fucked into the deep dark night, their grunts and moans mingled with the dog-like barks of black-crowned night herons.

It was close to six when Sam pulled his car out of St. Francis Village. Around the corner down Ahern Street he passed about twenty folks sitting on the sidewalk who would probably be sleeping on it tonight. He shuddered at the thought of sleeping on that cold cement with cardboard and a blanket for a bed. He felt anger and embarrassment at the country he loved, which allowed this level of poverty and homelessness to exist.

The different worlds he straddled were often bizarre in their contrasts, meeting with the most impoverished and disabled people and Sacramento's richest and most successful people within only minutes and blocks from each other. Hell, this was Friday and he was ready to escape into the world of friends, allies and margaritas.

Sam finally found a parking spot near Luna's Cantina at 16th and O Streets. He lit his pipe, taking a long hit of the skunky buds that were a friend's homegrown. One hit was just right. Then he put some drops in his eyes, closed them, and lowered his car seat back for about five minutes. He relaxed and enjoyed the high, which swept his thoughts deep into the day's events, his brain rehashing a few scenes.

Jake had come back to the Living Sober office late Thursday afternoon, much to his and Tony's surprise. He said he bought a bottle, took one drink and then felt disgusted with himself and threw it away. He decided at that moment that he'd try to get straight and enter the program.

With Jake starting recovery and his Board willing to lead a direct action, maybe something positive could come from Paul's senseless murder. Sam took a deep breath and hummed a quiet 'Om' for 30 seconds. He felt his shoulders relax and he entered a timeless, thoughtless place. Feeling a bit refreshed he climbed out of his car, payed the meter, and entered the brightly colored restaurant.

He saw Sheila smiling and laughing with her assistant director and good friend Debra near the entrance to the back of the bar where people at the Friday fundraiser were already in high spirits. A mariachi band played their guitars and sang lyrics in both English and Spanish. Sheila kissed Sam's cheek and he gave her a quick hug.

"I need a margarita quick, do you want anything to drink?"

She shook her head, adding, "I've got to be on until the intermission, then I'll be ready for a margy."

After grabbing his drink he spotted Kalen in a back corner deep in conversation with Carly. Sam waved and gave them their space while talking to some of Sheila's staff at the clinic, mostly younger women who liked to party after a hard week of work. Two of the women had worked for him at the Village as Jesuit Volunteers who dedicated a year of service at non-profits. Right out of college, they were bright and enthusiastic and the contacts they made usually helped them get paying jobs.

"Keep up the fight with White and Bright," one of

the girls teased Sam. He and Sheila's last names together sounded like a toothpaste commercial.

"White and Bright a smile's delight," Sam joked back.

"White and Bright is outta-sight!"

"Keep it tight all night with White and Bright." The women took turns in this banter that could go on for a while, but tonight they ended it there.

One of the young women who had worked at the Village said, "I can't believe that Paul Dixon was killed, how is everyone taking it?"

Sam said, "We're trying to hold things together. The guests are more frazzled than usual. The memorial service will be Wednesday; we've arranged for Paul's family from Kansas to be there. On Tuesday our Board is leading a sit-in at the Supervisor's offices in Paul's honor, but we're focusing on women and children." Just then Kalen walked over and asked the young staffers if he could steal Sam away for a minute.

Kalen had an arm around Sam as they walked to the back corner where Carly was waiting. "Hey, what about those Kings, Western Conference Champions!" Kalen said proudly as he high-fived Sam.

"Pretty exciting, they're good enough to win it all and

we got home court," Sam said, smiling. Carly nodded and smiled up at Sam as he sat down and they took sips of their drinks.

Kalen said in a low voice, "Good to see you brother. You holding up okay?"

Sam just held his hands out in front of him with his palms up as if to say, "Best I can under the circumstances."

"Carly told me about your meeting with Regina, what a dickhead! I'll be working on him for you, but I wanted to talk to you about Buck. He is really coming after you this time, Sam. He's been meeting with council members and the City Manager and his staff and pressing his case against the campers and the Village in general. He gave a speech to the North Sac Business Association on Monday and said he's started a political fund with his own money and he's raising more. It's almost like he expected the murder to happen and had his campaign apparatus primed and ready to go."

Sam shrugged. "So what's new?"

"I'm not kidding Sam, he's putting a lot of pressure on me to clear off the campers from the North side of the river and he's got Emerson the Sacramento Bee columnist doing his ranting for him. I think the column will come out tomorrow. He's been working on this for a while and he's using the murder to kick off his hate campaign."

Kalen looked at Carly who said, "At first I wasn't sure about your sit-in, but after meeting with Regina I think you're right to go on the offensive in a big way."

"I think you'll need all the help you can get," added Kalen. Sam thanked them for their assistance and they talked over the potential matchups in the upcoming local elections.

Later in the evening, her responsibilities over, Sheila sat with Sam and they drank a margarita. People were leaving and saying their goodbyes and one of Sheila's staff said, "Tonight's the night for White and Bright," and they laughed. Sheila thanked her remaining staff, the restaurant owner and employees, then they headed out to their cars.

"I think we hit our fundraising target of five thousand for the clinic!" said Sheila.

Sam nodded. "Nice event!"

As they walked he told her about Jake getting into rehab and meeting with the Supervisor.

"When you head to Oakland in the morning I'm going to try to talk with Charlie at the hospital. The homicide detective called me today and said Charlie's doctor cleared him for questioning, but he won't talk to them, so they asked for my help."

When they got to her car, Sheila held his hand and looked in his eyes. "I know you're hurting from this shooting, but maybe with Jake getting help and the sit-in, good things could come from it."

"I hope you're right."

———

Jake sat in a circle of twenty men and women at the Friday night AA meeting of the New Life housing program off Marysville Boulevard. They were packed in shoulder to shoulder. Jake trembled, sweating and ruminating. *I need a drink bad. I'm losing it. I feel like hell. I'll get through this meeting, but while everybody's BSing around afterward I'll sneak off. There's a liquor store eight blocks away.*

Tony Ruiz, founder of New Life began the meeting. "I'm Tony. I'm an alcoholic and a drug addict."

Everyone said in unison "Hello Tony."

Everyone, that is, except Jake and his roommate, the other new resident Chico, a wiry young man with hair in cornrows and gangster tats covering his neck and forearms.

Tony proudly said, "I've been sober for twelve years and every day sober is a blessing. When I drank and used I hurt everyone I loved and some I didn't. Through sobriety I have a family and a life. One day at a time we can make amends and rebuild our life."

Another older guy named Skip introduced himself and told of being a musician in a well-known local rock band and how he had lost almost everything behind cocaine and booze. He'd been sober for eight years and said he was often a sponsor for new people in the program. Others in the circle told brief stories and measured their sobriety in weeks or months instead of years.

Tony had warned Jake and Chico that they'd be expected to introduce themselves and to tell some of their story at the meeting.

The somber and steady Chico went first. "I ran with a north end gang and using was part of the culture. We sold crystal, crack, horse, weed, whatever we could get a hold of and I've been busted several times. I just got out of Folsom and I never want to go back. I want to stay straight and get out of the life." He ended by saying, "My old gang is probably looking for me, so you won't see me going out much."

Then it was Jake's turn. "You can call me shaky Jake tonight." People laughed. He told them about finding his young daughter in the pool. His voice cracked when he said he couldn't live with her loss. He thought about suicide constantly, and drank to get by. He described how he lost his job, his family, and had become homeless. He said, "I'll be honest, sitting here before the meeting started I was thinking about running out and getting something to drink afterwards. I think of my dead daughter in my arms and I just want to get obliterated. I think about the pain I've caused my wife and son and I just want to jump in the river and sink to the bottom."

"Fake it till you make it!" yelled one of the meeting participants and this got a few chuckles to break the tension.

"One day at a time," yelled another.

Most of the participants were wiping tears and Jake said, "I'm sorry to lay that on you, but it helped to say it."

After the meeting Tony brought Skip over to meet Jake. "Good to meet you Jake. In a few weeks you'll need to start attending some outside meetings and I'd like to invite you to one I go to in Midtown."

Jake wiped sweat from his face with a trembling hand. "I'm gonna need all the help I can get."

Skip talked to Jake about the friends he'd had to leave behind because they were using and how difficult it still was on some days when things weren't going his way. They talked for about half an hour and found out they had some common connections in the community.

Skip told Jake, "You've taken the first step in recognizing you have a problem, so hang in there and work the program." Jake nodded, but he was thinking, *Shit, I hope I can make it through the week.*

CHAPTER FOUR - BUCK SQUAWKS, CHARLIE TALKS

Saturday, April 13, 2002

Saturday morning Sam's day began with a cup of dark roasted coffee and his ritual reading of the Sacramento Bee. On the front page of the metro section he saw the opinion column titled:

CITY NEEDS TO BUCK UP AND CLEAN UP THE AMERICAN RIVER PARKWAY

BY JAVIER EMERSON

The latest incident of violent criminal behavior in the American River Parkway has ended with the shooting murder of one man and another man in the hospital. This example of lawlessness among the homeless transients camping illegally in our jewel of a parkway raises the question of the safety of legitimate park users. This writer recently accompanied local landowner and philanthropist Bill Buckmeister on a tour of some of the homeless camps along the American River. Many of these 'camps' were piles of disgusting filth and trash including empty bottles, pornography and hypodermic needles. Buckmeister railed at the City's lack of enforcement of the anti-camping laws: 'As long as the city tolerates this depravity and destruction of our parkway, this blight will continue and worsen.'

(Sam began to formulate his response letter to the *Bee*. He hated it when local journalists used the word "transients" to describe homeless people. All the data on Sacramento's homeless population showed that half had lived in the Sacramento region for over ten years and eighty to ninety percent had lived in Sacramento over a year. He pictured Buck wining and dining the columnist at some expensive restaurant before or after their "tour" of homeless camps.)

Of course, homeless advocates continue to blame a lack of affordable housing for the illegal camping, but this tired refrain is like pie in the sky. We're never going to solve the complicated problem of homelessness—we haven't yet—but we can solve the problem of illegal camping in our parkway by simply enforcing existing law. City Police and Park Rangers complain that they don't have the resources they need to adequately enforce the camping laws and that these hundreds of homeless campers will simply move into the downtown/midtown neighborhoods and parks. Buckmeister adds that he's 'tired of homeless magnets like St. Francis Village enabling the illegal and irresponsible behavior of addicts and criminals.'

(Sam knew Police and Park Rangers who would shake their heads at the notion of ending homeless camping simply by enforcement. When campers took their cases to court the City often lost and keeping homeless people in jail for non-violent offenses was a huge waste of money the city couldn't afford. Of course the constant camping citations did criminalize homeless people, many of whom suffered from addictions and mental illness.)

"I know I'll hear from people, like my former teacher and fellow Catholic Sister Julie Baldwin who works at St. Frances Village, that I'm being unkind or intolerant. But what we need here is some 'tough love' that will clean up our parkway jewel and in the process force some of these transients to go back where they came from or get jobs like the rest of us."

Sam sighed heavily as he put down the newspaper. This kind of misinformation was status quo. If you counted recycling, most homeless people had jobs, but were underemployed and couldn't afford housing even if they worked full time. He looked forward to their direct action campaign to frame the debate and get the truth out. Affordable, accessible housing with support services was the only real solution and it wasn't cheap, but it often paid for itself by keeping homeless folks out of hospitals, jails and mental health centers.

He finished writing his letter to the editor. He would let it sit and come back to it later when he wasn't so pissed off and maybe tone it down a bit. He took a deep breath and remembered that he was going to the hospital to see Charlie. He wasn't looking forward to it, but he hoped Charlie could and would talk to him.

Later that morning as Sam walked through the entrance to the hospital he noticed the cascading spring roses, blooming like red and yellow fireworks. Out of the corner of his eye he spotted Moreno slouched onto a large granite rock in the garden. Moreno, hair dusty and disheveled, grinned sheepishly as Sam approached.

"There's no loitering here you know," Sam joked.

Moreno said, "Sorry, I heard you were looking for me."

"Yeah. You look like shit, but at least you're still smiling. You know Jake has done a good thing getting in the program, right?"

"How's he doing? He seemed real serious this time."

"He's just working the program, going to meetings, and hanging out at New Life with the other folks in the program. You know we can get you in when you're ready bro."

Moreno shook his head. "I'm not a big program person you know, the army burnt that out of me. I like to do my own thing and I can quit when I feel like it."

It was Sam's turn to smile sadly and he asked Moreno if he'd been up to see Charlie.

"I tried to see him, but they're restricting his visitors and they asked if I was you because you were the only person on the list to see him. I've been waiting for you because I wanted you to know that there's a rumor on the street telegraph that Charlie told some other campers about Paul finding something, like a big stash, but it's not clear what he found. Charlie's big mouth might have gotten him and Paul shot."

"What?" said a surprised Sam. "That would make more sense than a random shooting."

"Maybe the killer got Paul to tell him where the stash is and didn't want the word to get around," said Moreno. "I've put the word out among friends to track down the folks that Charlie supposedly talked to. You know the street telegraph, it gets twisted, but there's usually some truth to it."

Sam nodded, "If the killer knows where it is why wouldn't he just go get it? Anyway, thanks for the info. I'll let the police know about the rumor, so they can check it out and let me know if you find out anything more. Now I need to see Charlie."

Moreno said, "Okay. I'm waiting for Cat to show up, she's my new camp partner."

Sam smiled at Moreno again and handed him a ten dollar bill. "Have some coffee and something to eat on me and if you stay sober I could take you two to see Jake after this."

"Okay, I'll meet you back here in about 45 minutes." Then Moreno whispered, "Good luck with Charlie, you know he ain't the brightest bulb, right?"

Sam stopped at the nurses' station to ask about Charlie's room, but they wouldn't give him the number until he showed them some ID. *That's good*, thought Sam, *Charlie may still be in danger if the rumor is true and the killer thinks he knows something.*

Sam opened the door, strong smells of antiseptic and body odors accosting him. Charlie had a room to himself. He was lying on his back with thick layers of gauze bandages covering the right side of his face. His left eye peeked out from under the wrap on his forehead and he seemed to be awake. He saw Sam and his eye watered up. He blinked away tears and motioned Sam to his left side.

Outside Charlie's room at a small desk used by non-nursing staff, a middle aged woman called her nephew who was paying her good money to keep an eye on the homeless guy's room.

"A big white guy in his forties just went into the guy's room," she whispered.

"Does he look like a cop?"

"No, I don't think so, he's wearing jeans and don't act like a cop. He must've been approved by the cops though. Some other homeless looking guy came by earlier, but they wouldn't let him in."

"Okay, thanks Auntie. You did good. Call me when he leaves, okay?"

Oblivious to the conversation in the hallway, Sam said, "Hey Charlie, glad to see you're conscious and breathing. Can you talk?" Charlie nodded slightly and Sam asked, "How are you? Can you hear me okay?"

Charlie said in a bare whisper, "Hurtsh ta talk. I'sh better dan Paul, can't believe he'sh gone. Dey shayin I may never shee agin wit ma right eye and ma ear hash a loud ringin that don't go way."

Sam shook his head side to side. "We all miss Paul and everyone from the Village sends you their love. I'm sorry you got caught up in this crazy shit Charlie."

Charlie's eye watered again. "It'sh prob'ly my fault, I

shot off my big mouf."

He beckoned Sam closer with his left hand (his right arm was stuck with IVs). Sam leaned down close to Charlie's head, his ear only inches from the injured man's lips. Charlie whispered, "He mate me promishe not a tell a shoul bout none a dish. I ain't told dem cops, but Paul found shumpin like a treasure wit gold up in a tree. I know shounds crazy, but he showed me. Twash a big honkin pieshe a gold da shize a ma thumb. Paul shaid they'sh plenty mo left in da tree. Paul had shome a da gold and he shold it. I got shitfashed wit da money he gave me and I tol' shomeone dat Paul found da money in shome shtash, I did'n tell em bout no gold I don't think, but I mighta shaid I knew where't wash. I'sh sho damn shtupid."

Sam kept his voice down and asked, "Do you know anything about where Paul found it or whether anyone hassled him about it?"

Charlie nodded faintly. "He shaid, 't wash in a big bent up five finger tree near Pardishe beash."

"Did he say where in the tree he found it?"

"He shaid twash up high in a hole. When he casht da gold, he tol' me shome guys in a black car grabbed 'im on the shtreet and hit 'im. They musht a know'd he had money. Paul took em to our camp and give dem 'bout twelf-hunred dollars. He wash shcared dat night."

"Do you know if that was all the cash Paul got?"

"No, he shent shome to hish folksh in Kanshash."

"Do you remember who you may have told about the gold?"

Charlie was silent for a long minute blinking and swallowing. Sam handed him his water with a straw and he drank. *I know I went to Dave and Jan's to score some crystal*, thought Charlie, *but I better not mention that.* "I can't amember," he finally said, but Sam thought he was holding back for some reason.

"Look Charlie, this is just between you and me and it might be important."

"Well, I do amember goin' to shee peoplesh on da Island, but I got meshed up and it'sh kinda a blur. I'shorry Sam, I might a got em kilt."

"Look Charlie, you were his best friend and you didn't shoot him, some greedy asshole did. You need to rest and get well, your information may help the cops find his killer. Are you cool with me telling the police about this? They'll want to talk to you soon and you should tell them about his finding gold in a tree at Paradise Beach and all the rest." Charlie nodded.

Sam asked Charlie if there was anything he needed and Charlie said, "I hope dey fine me a plashe da go when I have to leave. I'shcared to be out dere agin Sam."

Sam promised that he'd help Charlie find a safe place to live when he was discharged. Sam left his card with hospital staff and asked that he be contacted prior to Charlie's release.

Sam walked out of the hospital and had already dialed Police Captain Mike Ortega who was heading up the murder investigation. He told Ortega about his conversation with Charlie and about the stash of gold Paul had found in a large bent tree, "like a hand with fingers." He also told him about Paul cashing the nuggets, sending money to his family and how Paul got jumped soon after cashing the gold.

"Someone might have seen him at the gold cashing business," said Ortega.

"Yeah, Paul told Charlie that two guys in a black car beat him and made him take them to his camp. They robbed him of twelve hundred bucks."

"They robbed him? Or was he selling something?"

"Charlie said they robbed him and he was really scared."

"Thanks, it's good to have some leads to chase down. Charlie needs to talk to our investigators who will be coming over to the hospital soon. You sure he doesn't know where the stash is? I mean it sounds pretty crazy, this story."

"Charlie says he saw a piece of the gold the size of his thumb and Paul told him the tree was at Paradise Beach."

"Okay, we'll check out places he was likely to sell the gold and where he sent money and to whom, if he did. Thanks Sam, it's nice to have a motive to make some sense of this!" Ortega hung up.

Sam looked around for Moreno from the front of the hospital. He was thinking, *I might know the very tree Charlie was talking about near Paradise Beach, but it can't be the same tree can it?* He lived in the River Park neighborhood about eight blocks from the trailhead to Paradise Beach. He and some friends met for full moon drum circles during the warmer months and they usually drummed out by an old twisted tree with branches that looked like a hand in a low lying ravine a stone's throw from the river.

He took Kabu out to the beach for runs several times a week, so he knew the area well. He thought, *I've sat in that old tree many times*. It did seem like the palm of a giant hand. It could be in any one of a hundred trees near Paradise Beach, but the description was pretty specific.

Sam found Moreno sitting with Cat on the lawn of Sutter's Fort under towering elm trees across the street from the hospital.

"Hey Oretha" said Sam.

"Hey Sam, how's Charlie doin'?"

"His head is all wrapped up, but he could talk to me. They say he's lost his right eye. Moreno and I had talked about going to see Jake, You want to go too?"

Cat nodded and they loaded their bikes into the back of Sam's electric Ford truck, then squeezed into his front seat. He pulled out of his parking space on 28th Street and Moreno commented on how quiet the truck was. They didn't see the low-riding, tricked-out small black Honda with heavily tinted windows pull out behind them.

"So what did Charlie have to say, Sam?" asked Moreno as they drove up the onramp and headed to north Sacramento.

"Do you mind if I wait and go over it with Jake too? The short version is that Charlie confirms that Paul found a stash of gold, if you can believe it," Sam said shaking his head.

"No fucking way!" said Oretha looking at Moreno with large eyes.

"Did Charlie know where it was?" asked Moreno.

"Not exactly," replied Sam.

"¡Ay Dios mío!" Moreno said in a reverent tone and crossed himself.

They pulled up outside the New Life residential program, which looked like most of the other boxy eight-unit apartment buildings in the area, though it was better maintained with newish green trim and brown exterior paint. They went to the manager's door and knocked. The door opened quickly and a burly black man with a bald head and thick beard with specks of white smiled broadly.

"Well, I'll be!" he said in a deep coarse voice. "Hi, Mr. White. What can I do for you all?"

"Hey Deon," Sam replied. "We're here to visit with Jake and these are his good friends Moreno and Oretha."

"Let me call Jake and have him come meet with you

down here in the patio. You know we usually don't allow visitors this early in his recovery, but I'll make an exception with you."

A few minutes later Jake stepped shakily down each stair grasping the banner tightly with his right hand. He hugged Moreno saying, "Good to see you bro."

Moreno said, "You look like shit, are you okay?"

Jake chuckled weakly and shook hands with Sam. "The DTs have been kicking my ass"—he held out his left hand to show it was visibly shaking—"but it's finally getting a little better. What's your excuse?" Jake said, squinting at Moreno. Jake hugged Oretha and said, "Thanks for coming."

Sitting in plastic chairs in the cement courtyard, Moreno told Jake that he and Cat were camping together now. Jake smiled at Oretha the whole time and he could swear she blushed.

Sam told Jake that it should remain confidential, but shared that he had gone to see Charlie and that Charlie confirmed the rumor that Paul had found some gold near the river. "He says he saw two big chunks of gold and even held them in his hand. He also feels guilty because he may have told someone about Paul finding the gold when he was high."

Jake whistled. "Goddamn, unbelievable. At least it makes more sense now, but poor Charlie has to live with the guilt that he might have got his buddy killed."

"Does Charlie know where Paul found it?" asked Moreno again.

"Paul told him it was in a big old tree shaped like a hand down by the river," said Sam, leaving out the part about Paradise Beach. He didn't want word to get out and have all kinds of people searching for it. "Charlie said that Paul cashed two pieces of gold, but he doesn't know where. He said after Paul cashed the gold, he sent most of the money to his family in Kansas. After that Paul was jumped by some guys in a black car who beat him and forced him to give them the money he'd stashed in camp. They got about twelve hundred bucks Charlie thinks."

"Wow," said Jake and Mota at the same time. "Now it's coming together, shit!" said Jake.

Just then Jake heard a loud "Pssssttt" that came from the window of his apartment upstairs and he looked up to see the curtains parted.

He said, "Just a second I think my roommate needs something." He slowly climbed the stairs. While Jake was gone, Sam remembered what Charlie had told him about where he went the night Paul cashed the gold.

Looking intently at Moreno and Oretha he said, "Charlie told me he went to the island after Paul gave him some money. I think he remembers who he told, but he didn't want to tell me. He said he got really messed up and couldn't remember."

Oretha and Moreno glanced at each other and then turned back to Sam.

"What?" Sam asked.

Moreno spoke first. "We were just out on the island yesterday and this couple Dave and Jan are the ones who told us they had heard the rumor of Paul finding a stash. They deal and that's probably where Charlie went with his money. He didn't want to tell you that he was going there to buy crystal."

"So you think this couple Jan and Dave got Charlie high, got the info and told someone else?" asked Sam.

"Jan's a total space case," said Oretha, "Dave's the one who seems to get the dope and manage the business."

Moreno nodded, "Cat's right, Dave has some connections to get the dope on a regular basis and he could have told someone about the gold hoping to get paid for the info or just to get in good with his connection. Without the exact location it might not be worth much. Dave is more together than Jan, but he's homeless and strung out too. No telling what he'd do for dope."

Jake came back and in a low voice said, "My roommate is freaked because he was looking out the window and saw a parked car close by that he's sure is driven by some of his former gang buddies. He thought they were watching this building. He's just a week out of prison trying to stay straight, and he thinks his gang is looking for him. They're worried he might snitch them out to the cops."

Sam asked, "What kind of car is it?"

"He said it was a black Honda."

"I thought I saw a black Honda park right after we pulled up." Moreno said.

"I didn't notice them at all," said Sam. "Look Jake we have to go, I just wanted to check in on you. I ran into Moreno and Oretha on my way over and I knew they'd want to see you too. I'm so glad you're hanging in with the program, the first week is always tough."

"I miss you're smiling face out there bro, but I'm proud of you. Hang in there!" said Moreno and they hugged goodbye.

Oretha said, "Good luck Jake, let us know what its like to be sober."

"I'll be honest," said Jake, "half the time I got a foot out the door and I'm thinking about where I can score some booze, but people here keep pulling me back. We talk a lot and take it one day at a time. We'll see."

Sam hugged Jake goodbye. He then knocked on Deon's door again and told him what had transpired with Jake and his roommate. "If the car stays there after we pull out you better call the cops. Do you know what gang Jake's roommate was in?"

"It's the Beasties in North Sac. I don't know them, but he says they're bad dudes. He's kind of hiding out here, so them showing up could be dangerous. Thanks for the heads up." Deon locked the gate behind them.

Sam, Oretha and Moreno got in Sam's truck and pulled away from the curb. Sam hung a U turn and passed the Honda on the way out of the neighborhood. They could see the silhouettes of two guys in the front seat, but the windows were heavily tinted and they couldn't make out their faces. They turned right onto Marysville Boulevard and before they got to the next intersection Sam noticed the black Honda in the rear-view mirror. It turned the corner and headed in their direction.

"It looks like they're following us," said a surprised Sam.

"I'm thinking they followed us from the hospital, so they must be watching Charlie." Oretha said, "I didn't want to mention it back there, but my older brother had some connections to the Beasties. He sold dope for them. When they sink their claws into you, you're screwed."

"I've got an idea," said Sam. He knew the Marysville Boulevard police station was up ahead. "You guys aren't holding are you?"

Moreno said, "Just a little pot, they don't call me Mota for nothing."

Sam said, "Leave it in the car," he turned on his right signal and pulled into the police station parking lot.

PART TWO

CHAPTER FIVE - A DEAD MAN'S STORY

Sunday, April 7, 2002 - Sacramento's American River Parkway

Tinker woke up to Charlie's snoring and watched dew drops drip from the edge of the tarp strung between two trees. They turned to diamond sparkle as they fell through a golden ray of early sun. He had to pee badly, so he unzipped his sleeping bag and climbed out in his socks and underwear, ducking under the tarp to piss at the base of a tree.

"Ah!" he sighed. The clear blue sky seemed to hold endless promise and he shouted at Charlie, "Ged up Challi, es Sundy, time fo' donuts en drenken.'"

A bleary, wrinkled face appeared from under his sleeping bag and Charlie blinked bloodshot eyes at Tinker. From deep in his throat rumbled something between a grunt and a growl. Charlie was a man of few words and he was hungover most mornings. They both liked to drink, but Charlie drank more than Tinker, which was saying something. He'd burned out a lot more brain cells than Tinker having been an alcoholic since his teens, but he understood Tinker better than anyone, except maybe Tinker's father. In turn Tinker supported him with his monthly disability check, though Charlie made a little money recycling.

They cleaned up a bit, got on their bikes and pedaled for the donut shop on 16th Street. Riding over the pedestrian bridge they squinted into the bright morning sun as their heads pounded. Donuts were a Sunday ritual when they had money; so was a stop at the liquor store down the street. Tinker bought them a bottle of cheap whiskey and a couple Pabst beers, as it was still early in the month. Later in the month it would be a bottle of Thunderbird. They pedaled back to the river with the whiskey and beer chasers.

Sundays tended to be a day of peace from the cops patrolling camps along the river and it was safer to drink in public. They sat in some shade with their backs against a fallen log and passed the bottle back and forth.

Charlie started shaking, as usual, laughing to himself.

Tinker looked at him and mouthed "What?"

He shook his head laughing and Tinker read his lips: "That guy last night falling over." He made a tumbling motion with his hands and Tinker laughed with him, remembering the guy on a bike who they'd drunk with the night before at a neighbor's camp.

When the guy tried to leave he only got about ten feet before falling on top of his bike and they'd watched him do this over and over until he finally gave up and tried to walk his bike, only to fall over it again. This cracked everyone up even worse. The poor guy was still lying passed out in the bushes next to his bike when he and Charlie had left.

They were laughing hard together and Tinker lip read Charlie again as he said, "Snake and Mota prob'ly heped 'em out."

Tinker nodded. Some people got real mean when they got drunk, but Charlie, he just got goofy, laughing easily and talking a little more than usual, which still wasn't much. Tinker was mostly like Charlie, but sometimes he would get agitated and at times really pissed off.

Tinker was drunk already by midday. They'd eaten some bread and peanut butter and when he stood up to pee he got light headed and fell right back down.

Charlie looked at him and said, "You dummy."

Tinker's face contorted in anger. He got up shakily and yelled spitting in Charlie's face, "Fack wu! Wu da dummy! Wu da dummy!" Tinker saw the shock on his friend's face, though it was numbed by the whiskey and beer, Charlie was truly surprised by his anger.

Tinker couldn't really hear him say "dummy"—he had less than 5% of his hearing and he hadn't been able to speak much when he was a kid. But that didn't stop him from "listening" in his own way, and the one word he could lip read anytime was "dummy." He'd been called a dummy so often as a child and a young worker that this one word still cut him like a knife. Tinker saw red.

When he came back to himself, Charlie was trying to lean away from him and had his hands up in self-defense. Tinker realized his fists were clenched and his right hand raised, ready to hit Charlie.

He dropped his hand, shook his head and got up. Looking down at Charlie he said, "Don' evah caw me dummy! Ah see wu a comp lateh." He relieved himself and got on his bike, which was hitched to a small bike trailer full of his stuff. He pedaled away from a startled and confused Charlie. Riding down a dirt track along the levee, he headed under the 80 freeway, still pissed off. Whiskey-fed rage boiled inside him.

He had always felt like the outsider, watching other boys and girls talking and laughing. He'd had a little speech and sign language training while in school, but could barely read and write as a kid. He'd grown up in Kansas outside a small farm town. His father was deaf, dumb and illiterate, but he was the hardest worker you ever saw. He always took on the dirtiest, most difficult jobs and he was honest as the day was long.

It was just the two of them, and at fourteen Tinker had dropped out of school to help his dad work. They worked odd jobs together for over twenty-five years. Tinker was always good at fixing things with whatever was at hand, so he and his dad were a good team.

His mother could hear and speak, but she left them when he was two. He couldn't really remember his mother except from the one photograph she left behind. He thought, *I must have got my mom's quick temper and bad back.*

Tinker's dad was in great shape and could outwork men half his age. Though he was branded with the nick name "Dummy" by the local farmers and there were always pranks, the old man's good nature had allowed him to take it all in stride, always smiling. Tinker didn't have his dad's patience so when they called him a dummy and he saw it, they were in for a fight.

He had slowly taught himself to read and reading was his escape from a life of hard work and now from life on the streets. He still couldn't speak most of the words he'd learned to read because he couldn't hear what they sound like, so most people assumed he was stupid and he didn't mind playing dumb most of the time.

Charlie knew he was a lot smarter than he let on because he saw him reading often. Charlie was illiterate himself, but he was a friend Tinker could trust to have his back, at least when he wasn't too wasted.

Pedaling his heavy load, Tinker's heart pounded, but it felt good to sweat out some of the alcohol. His anger had subsided. He thought of Paradise Beach where kids drink and smoke and girls were in bikinis. He loved Paradise Beach, but Charlie just liked to hang out not far from camp and drink. He thought maybe it wasn't fair, leaving Charlie like that, but he was enjoying a break from his buddy.

Tinker reveled in the thick, green grass of early April

and the huge trees covered with budding leaves and flowers. The smells of the river filled his nose and made him smile. He had sharp eyesight and a sense of smell better than most. These senses helped him survive. Thin clouds spread across the sky that made him think of fish skeletons or bird wings.

He pushed his rig from the top of the levee down through the thick sand to the beach. The river ran high in April. He was on the edge of the Paradise beach inlet, where kids from high schools or students from the nearby college hung out. They played volleyball or slung skim boards into tiny river swells. God, he loved this California weather and the beach scene.

He didn't fit with this crowd, so he stayed on the sidelines of the action. Later in the afternoon when everyone was drunk or high he would work his way over to the main beach in hope of buying a little pot or at least having a joint passed his way. He slept soundly in the shade of a thicket for over an hour and woke up in a sweat as the sun had shifted and was now burning his neck and right ear.

He moved away from the beach and sat under a broad gnarly tree that twisted in the direction of the river's flow. Looking up he saw five or six branches that looked like a giant hand. Pulling his frayed copy of "Tom Sawyer" and a duct taped Webster's paperback dictionary out of his bike trailer, he laid back against an uncovered tree root. After reading for a while he climbed the thick bent trunk until he was about six feet off the ground and sat on a level section where the row of large branches began to grow upward. He rested on this natural bench, his whole body fitting in what felt like the palm of a hand. The old tree's giant roots were exposed, arcing under the sand like sea serpents.

The sun was low in the sky when he wandered over to the main beach and scoped out who was smoking. A group of mostly brown kids were passing a joint and he walked up smiling, pressing his right thumb and forefinger together he raised them to his lips. They smiled back and one of them passed him the joint. After taking a long drag he passed it to the next in line.

One of the kids said something to him, but he only caught the last two words by lip reading "old man." He pointed to his ears and shook his head as he often did to let people know he was deaf and they seemed to understand.

Opening his hand to reveal a twenty dollar bill he said, "Con ah buy?" They looked at each other and the guy who seemed to be the leader of the group looked around carefully then dug into his backpack and showed him a small baggie with some green buds, so he handed him the twenty.

Tinker walked back towards the tree. Behind him the sun's reflection bounced off the river like a mirror doubling its blinding golden rays. As he looked up into the branches of the big twisted tree a bright glint of sun caught his eye. When he got closer he spotted the small reflection as if shiny metal was embedded high in a branch of the tree. He was curious, but climbed back up onto the bench of the tree and read for an hour as the beach crowd thinned out.

After watching the sun sink behind the trees across the river, he remembered the glinting object and thought he would take a look. The middle branches grew close together with smaller branches growing outward that he could climb almost like a ladder. He pulled himself up to a point where he could see a couple inches of shiny metal framed by a round hole of thick bark.

He climbed down to his bike trailer and dug out a

rubber mallet, claw hammer and a large wood chisel from his tools. Even though he didn't make much money doing it, he loved fixing something broken or building something useful. He climbed back up into the tree with the tools jammed into his leather belt. He also brought some heavy rope that he used to tie himself off to the main branch to free his hands and he began to chisel away at the edges of the hole. More metal revealed itself as each chunk of bark was cut away. His heart thumped in his chest as the metal object began to look like some kind of heavy iron box.

He had to chisel at it for a while before his fingers could grab the end of the box and he imagined he was doing some kind of organ removal. It was getting dark, but he was slowly working the box loose from the grip of the old tree. Most people had left the beach and the two or three folks remaining were walking their dogs farther down river and didn't seem to be paying him any attention. The rubber mallet had deadened the pounding noise and no one had walked over to check him out. Finally working the heavy box out of its hole he saw another box wedged under it the exact same size.

Tinker's heart almost jumped out of his throat as

he examined the thick box which was closed by sturdy latches, though they had rusted badly.

"Shit! Mus be ten poun!" he said out loud. He untied his rope and clutched the box in one arm as he slowly climbed down. He balanced the box between his legs and sat on the bench of the tree trunk. He was able to knock the latches loose and pry open the box a little with his hammer. The lid groaned slowly as it opened and his breath came in gulps. Tears flooded into his eyes as he stared open mouthed at gold nuggets and small bottles of dust in the box he held.

Shaking badly he found a piece of animal hide rolled up on top. *Hell, must be gold, its fuckin' heavy,* he thought. He unrolled what felt like deerskin and saw lettering burned onto the inside.

PROPERTY OF MICHAEL O'CONNOR 1850

"Goddam!" he blurted, doing the math, "hunnert fitty years! No Way!" He rolled the skin back up and put it back in the box. He craned his neck to look around, but was relieved to see no one close.

He took some deep breaths to slow his heart down and tried to quit shaking. Taking out two nuggets, one the shape of his thumb and another round flat piece he put them in his pocket. A wave of fear swallowed him and he looked around for some time wondering what to do. He couldn't believe this was actual gold though it sure felt like what he'd imagined gold to be. Since it had been hidden here for so long maybe he should leave it a bit longer. It seemed a lot safer than carrying it all with him and he couldn't cash any on a Sunday night.

He remembered seeing "Cash for Gold" signs at one of the check cashing places he used and decided he would bring it there in the morning and see if it was real. He put the box back into the tree, not even checking the one under it. He covered up the boxes with some rags and wedged pieces of bark he found on the ground into the opening, constantly looking around so much that his neck hurt. He tapped them lightly with his mallet and thought, *If it's real, I come back soon.*

He rolled a joint and smoked some to calm himself. Then he pedaled back to their camp in the dark, a flashlight taped to the handlebars to light the dirt trail. He was still a little shaky, so he breathed deeply, taking in the smells of the river. He had to tell somebody, so when he got back to camp he grabbed Charlie's arm and pulled him into their little storage tent.

Charlie asked, "Are you still mad at me?"

Tinker shook his head, looked into his muddy brown eyes and said, "Pwomise wu won' tell nobody."

Charlie shook his head and said, "What?"

Tinker stuck out his hand and opened it to show his friend the two nuggets. "Ah see box up twee. Pawadise Beaj. Ah dig wit hammah."

Charlie held a piece in each hand, feeling their heft and rubbing their smooth surfaces between his thumb and fingers. He pointed at one piece with the index finger of his other hand. "You found? In tree?" he asked in disbelief. Tinker nodded expressively.

He didn't sleep too well that night, but when he did he dreamed of driving around in his own fancy car and pulling up to a big house with a large front door and a white wood fence.

Monday morning Tinker told Charlie more about finding the gold in the tree and made him promise again not to tell anyone.

"Aftew I cash da goad I go ovah to da vil and tell Don wad I foun'. He wi' hep me." Charlie went off to the Village to get lunch and Tinker pedaled into North

Sacramento where he remembered seeing a **CASH FOR GOLD** sign in the window of a check cashing place he'd used. He locked his bike and went inside. He waited in line and when his turn came he pulled the gold nuggets out of his pocket and rubbed his thumb and forefinger together in the sign that most folks recognize as money or cash.

The guy who ran the place was an older white man with gray hair and glasses covering baggy eyes that looked at him skeptically. When Tinker handed him the gold nuggets the man looked up at him in surprise.

"Where did you find this?"

Tinker read his lips but played dumb, shaking his head and pointing to his ears.

The man tried again and said slowly "Where? Where from?" Tinker just shook his head again and held out his hands as if to say *I don't understand.* The gray-haired guy got frustrated and shook his head, but he took the gold and pointed to a sign that had the word "gold" and a large figure of five hundred and ninety dollars per ounce written on it. Tinker nodded that he understood.

The man walked into an adjoining room and re-turned with a receipt book and four thousand, seven-hundred, and twenty dollars in cash. Tinker felt his heart jump and looked closely at the receipt he was handed, which had the cash figure and another figure of 8 ounces.

The man motioned for him to sign the bottom of the receipt and put his hand to his ear as if he was holding a phone: "Phone and address too." Tinker signed his name and then again shook his head as if he was confused and pushed the book back across the counter. The man tore off the top receipt and handed it to him with the cash, shaking his head and looking disgusted. Tinker count-ed the money, stashed the thick wad in his pocket, and walked out. His heart pounded like a jackhammer and he took deep breaths as he left the building.

He sat for a while on a wall by his bike and gear. He'd never had this much money in his hands, which shook as he worried about getting mugged. Then an idea came to him and he walked back into the check cashing building to use their money wire service. The man said Tinker needed to write down his address and the address where he wanted the money sent.

He used the Dignity Park address at the Village, wrote his dad's address in Kansas and paid the twelve dollars to wire him three thousand dollars with a short note that he was okay in Sacramento and wanted his dad to have this money. Tinker's dad couldn't read it, but his wife could. Almost ten years ago his father had remarried, which is when Tinker had left Kansas because three people was one too many in his dad's little cabin.

He felt elated when he got back on his bike and pedaled down Del Paso Boulevard toward their camp. He was thinking that the rest of the gold must be worth a fortune. He could afford to rent a place or maybe even buy a house, but then he remembered that his disability checks might get cut off. Disability had been his lifeline for the last ten years. He had to think this through and ask Don at the park to help him, but he felt so giddy it was hard to think straight.

Pedaling near the end of Del Paso Boulevard where the camps began, he noticed a black Honda with tinted windows. It had passed him a few minutes ago and was now parked on his side of the road. The windows came down as he approached and a muscled black arm with a yellow bandana tied around it was waving. He guessed the wave was meant for him since he was the only one there. He slowed down. He saw the other passenger also had a yellow bandana. He smelled the strong aromas of pot and meth and recognized the signs. Guys like this often came into the camps to harass and rob campers, especially early in the month when people got their checks.

They were saying something to him, but he didn't want to look too closely. He pointed at his ears, shook his head and rode past them. He swerved off the paved street onto the dirt shoulder. They drove up alongside him and the passenger, a smaller Hispanic guy, flashed a pistol and motioned for him to pull over. He saw a narrow foot trail branch off to the right into heavy brush, so he pedaled as hard as he could down the trail where the car couldn't follow.

He heard the doors open and was about twenty yards away from the car when he felt the concussion of a shot that hit a tree branch right over his head and he pedaled for all he was worth. He thought, *Thank God the trail turns into trees and hanging vines—they can't see me.* Tinker rode hard for five minutes until he intersected the bike trail. It seemed safer because cars weren't allowed on it and the park rangers often patrolled here.

I dodged a bullet all right. I can't believe these guys are after me so soon after cashing the gold. Maybe it's not the gold…? I didn't see them in the building or in the parking lot, but they found me awfully quick. He rode to camp and immediately stashed all but $200 of his money in the two caches Charlie and he shared.

He sat thinking hard about what he should do. He felt shaky and looked in Charlie's tent for something to drink. There was a wine bottle with several good slugs in it, so he gulped it down. He thought, *I better ride over to the Village to find Charlie and talk to Don at Dignity Park. Don will help me.*

Keeping to the trail, he approached the bridge that would take him over the river. He pulled into the brush and scoped it out. *If they're still looking for me this is a place they would expect me to cross.* He didn't see anyone except the usual line of folks riding their bikes or pulling carts and felt lucky there was no car access near here.

He thought, *Lunch at the Village is over by now. Too bad, I'm so hungry, but it will be easier to talk to staff.* He pedaled across the bridge and turned onto Beamer Street, four blocks east of the Village.

Suddenly, the same two guys jumped out of the Honda right in front of him, cutting him off. They had parked between a van and a truck and he didn't see them until it was too late.

They grabbed Tinker from both sides and the smaller guy stuck a gun in his ribs. The bigger guy slapped him hard on the right side of his head. They pulled him off his bike, dragged him over to their car and shoved him into the back seat. He looked frantically to see if anyone was nearby. There was usually a steady flow of foot and bike traffic on this street, but he never saw anyone.

The little guy climbed into the back seat next to him and elbowed him in the jaw. The big guy punched him hard in the ribs before taking the wheel. He was trying to cover up and roll with the punches, but the blows stunned him and hurt like hell.

The little guy pointed to Tinker's eyes and then at his own lips, saying slowly, "Two things or you die." He held up two fingers, then made the slashing sign across his throat. "One"—he held up one finger—"give me your money now."

Tinker didn't hesitate, he reached into his pocket and handed him the two hundred dollars, then held out his hands to the side to indicate this was all he had. The gunman pressed the gun into Tinker's left eye and shook his head. The big guy punched him hard on the breastbone and the air went out of him.

Tinker wheezed, "comp, comp, my comp" and he pointed to the North.

"I want all the money!" Tinker nodded vigorously. "Two"—the gunman held up two fingers—"Where is gold?"

Tinker gave him his most sincere look of confusion and innocence and shook his head "No mo, no mo!"

He looked at Tinker hard and said slowly, "Where did you find gold?"

"Ah steal, from house."

Looking confused the gunman said, "Take us to your camp, I want money, or you die." His hand slashed his throat more violently this time.

Tinker directed them up 16th Street to the Northgate off ramp. He pointed them to a dirt parking spot closest to the camp. They parked and grabbed him roughly, pushing him out of the car. He thought, *This might be private property and with any luck the cops or security dicks will show up and I can get away. If no one helps I'll take them to camp and give them the one thousand dollar stash and hope they don't kill me. If it looks like they want to kill me, I can still buy some time and say I know where more gold is.*

The little one just kept sneering at him saying, "No bullshit! Asshole," or something like that. He lead them down the worn foot trail through high grass and thick green brush, hoping that they'd run into a camper that he knew. One look at these guys and they would know something bad was up. He was thinking, *Shit after such good luck it sure swung around quickly to kick me in the ass. Hell it's even worse. Homeless is bad enough, but no one was trying to kill me.*

They passed a camp that looked abandoned, but he knew there were a couple folks camping in the bushes beyond the open meadow area and hoped they were watching through the branches. Snake and Mota were often nearby and they were men to be reckoned with. Even if they were high they'd know what to do. He prayed they were here somewhere.

They finally made it to his camp, but no one had come to his rescue. The yellow bandanas yanked him around and pushed him every few steps. Cuts in his mouth were bleeding. It hurt to breathe. He went right to the stash with one thousand dollars and dug it out from under a rock. He handed it to the little guy, who counted it with a smug smile across his face. He grabbed Tinker's chin, pushed his head back and looked into his eyes.

"If I find out you're holding back, you are dead." Tinker nodded his understanding and felt the relief flow over him as they turned around and left the way they had come.

His thoughts raced, *I don't care about the money. Hell, I got a lot more where that came from, but how did these guys know my business so fast? It must have been the old guy at the check cashing place or someone who was in the building when I was there. I didn't like that old guy, but how would he know gangsters?*

Charlie came back a while later and Tinker told him what happened, including the details of the black Honda and yellow arm bands. Charlie was more freaked out than he was.

He asked fearfully, "You brought them to our camp?"

Tinker replied angrily, "Yeah ow de kill me." He went to the other stash, dug out the $500 dollars he had left and gave fifty bucks to Charlie. They debated moving their camp, but decided the gangsters got what they wanted and wouldn't bother to come back. He wouldn't be cashing any more gold at that check cashing place.

Charlie went off to get fucked up as he always did when he had some money. He'd probably score some crystal and buy a couple bottles of whiskey. Tinker felt wiped out and every time he moved pain shot through his chest. He hadn't slept much the night before, so he crashed out for a nap. When he woke up it was too late to go to the Village to talk with Pastor Don. He was starving, so he walked to Jalisco's Tacos, which was close, cheap and good eats. He ate two large chicken burritos.

After eating he painfully walked back to where he had abandoned his bike and trailer and as he'd suspected they were gone. Then he walked over to Dignity Park and he could see through the locked fence that the bike was there. He was relieved that someone brought it there for safekeeping. He tracked down the evening watchman who knew him and let him into the Park to get his bike, but he left his trailer of tools.

He bought a six pack of Pabst blue ribbon and drank one as he pedaled back to camp. He was thinking about the high of finding the gold and the low of being beaten and robbed, all in two days. He had discovered a one hundred fifty year old treasure and the danger it could bring him.

PART THREE

CHAPTER SIX - PARASITES SUCK!

Monday, April 9, 2002

Franklin Golding sat at a round table with his hands resting on the white tablecloth. The other five chairs were empty. It was one of about fifteen tables set for the breakfast meeting of the North Sacramento Business Association. He stared at the folded name card: "Frank Golding, NSBA Member." His watch read seven-fifteen.

Conferences on Monday morning? Who's the fucking genius who came up with that? he thought as he watched the members shuffle into the Sequoia Room of the Sacramento Employment Agency building on Del Paso Boulevard.

He had arrived early to get a seat facing the stage. He knew he was not the most popular guy at the Association, which had a larger share of younger, more liberal business owners. He didn't like most of these dickhead yuppies and he wasn't about to get up to glad-hand anybody, but his membership helped him look legit. He had come to hear Bill "Buck" Buckmeister who was the keynote speaker for the monthly event.

He and Buck attended some of the same fundraisers together; their families went way back in Sacramento, too. Buck's dad and his uncle had been friends, though Buck was a bit younger than him and so wealthy now that he ran in circles high above Golding's rank.

Still, he was one of the celebrities in town that Golding usually agreed with and jealously looked up to. As the other tables started to fill, a couple of young black men came over to his table and asked if the chairs were available.

He thought, *Fuck no! Why do the negroes come to my table*, but instead he said, "Suit yourself."

They exchanged the usual pleasantries. One of them worked for City Councilman Kalen Jones, and a smiling Golding said, "I supported the other guy in the election."

The other man, who represented the Young Republicans, said, "Good for you!"

When most people had arrived and taken a seat, Buck came through the crowd smiling and shaking hands, self-confident like a shark in a school of fish. He didn't make it to their table, but when he looked their way Golding waved and Buck waved back smiling.

Buck was introduced by the president of the business association as a member, land owner, philanthropist and businessman. He thanked Buck for his support and willingness to share with them his thoughts on the topic of "Business Impediments" this morning.

Buck stood tall behind the dais, his shoulders back, chin jutting forward. "Thanks for having me here Jim." He nodded at the association president. "It's good to be back in North Sac, and North Sac is back!" The crowd clapped. "I'm going to focus on two impediments to business. The first is familiar ground and that is the long, expensive, twisted, and unreasonable building permit process in our city and county." Buck went on to castigate the environmental review process and to push for the streamlining of the building permit process. By the response he was getting from this crowd he knew they were very supportive of these positions. Next he moved on to what he termed the "Bum Problem."

"Let's be honest," he said, "these homeless bums choose to be outside, they don't want to work—and why?

Because they are irresponsible drug addicts and drunks supported by our tax dollars and they are coddled by do-gooder agencies like St. Frances Village. These criminals are allowed to camp on private property and in our once beautiful river parkway where they create huge piles of trash and filth. On one of my properties not far from here I've had to pay to remove tons of trash including old couches, mattresses, tarps, clothing, pornography, used needles and human excrement."

The response from the audience was mixed. Some hardliners like Golding were nodding and grunting in agreement, but others were shifting nervously in their seats. There were a few who volunteered at the Village or other homeless programs and most had probably contributed money to the Salvation Army, Volunteers of America and other non-profits. A few had family members, friends, or past acquaintances that were homeless or had been a paycheck away from losing their housing.

Undaunted, Buck plowed forward. "The homeless programs over-concentrated in the Richards Boulevard area, particularly St. Frances Village, have blighted the area so badly as to make it almost impossible for businesses to thrive in the neighborhood. They give people free food with no strings attached and then send them off to downtown and North Sac to crap in our alleyways, parks and private property. Police and Park Rangers aren't enforcing our anti-camping laws, which have been on the books since the gold rush era. Sure, they give citations and move people along when too many are in one spot, but these bums just want their cheap wine and drugs and they'll rob and steal to get them. Most of them belong behind bars, but instead we give them free camping in our most beautiful park, which is no longer safe for tax-paying citizens.

"Look, for all the money that goes to these enabling programs, homelessness only seems to get worse. Why? Because these bums don't want housing or work, they want hand outs and they want to get high, period. We need to put pressure on the enablers. We need some "Tough Love" that holds these bums and the programs that support their bad habits accountable.

"I've formed a 'Clean Up Our River Parks!' fund, seeded with $5,000 of my own money, that you can contribute to if you agree with me, and I've brought with me a petition to the city and county to force St. Frances Village to cap the number of meals they serve to 200 per day. It also requires the police to do their job and enforce the anti-vagrant, anti-camping and anti-drug laws. I hope you'll consider joining this effort."

Golding stood to applaud, whipped a $100 bill from his pocket, and waved it in the air. He was joined by about a fourth of the people there. Others swiveled nervously in their chairs and talked in low voices.

The councilman's aide said, "So much for Christian kindness." He got up and left the table.

Later Monday morning Golding leaned back in his chair, feet up on the desk, and stared at his framed city business license that read "Franklin Golding Enterprises." It had been a busy morning at his payday loan and check cashing business and he felt every bit as old as his sixty-four years. If all went well, this would be his last year running the business. He planned to sell it and retire at sixty-five—though truth be told, he could have retired years ago if it wasn't for his gambling debts.

He smiled smugly at his profitable morning. It was ironic that after hearing Buck's speech he'd met that deaf homeless bum with the beautiful nuggets who had been so easy to rip off.

Shit, the gold he brought in weighed more than twice

what I paid him. I was lucky I was at the front counter. It's the easiest five grand I've ever made.

Staring at the two gold nuggets on his desk he thought, *One nugget isn't all that unusual, I've bought quite a few over my thirty years in business, but two of this size and quality really makes me wonder where the guy got them. Sure, some are found or mined by small time river bank sluice operations and some are stolen, but I have a feeling about this.* When he was a kid his uncle had told him about the legend of lost gold hidden in a bent tree by the American River. It was supposedly stashed by a for-ty-niner who was killed before he could come back for it.

His uncle had run a pawn shop in North Sacramen-to for over thirty years and the lost gold was one of his uncle's favorite stories. His dad and he had worked at the shop; in fact he'd inherited the building from his uncle. He had changed the business to be much more profit-able, especially when you counted all the under-the-table money.

As a boy he had always dreamed of finding the treasure and spent much time riding his bike to the river searching for the old bent tree. The river was his escape from a drab and angry North Sacramento home where his mom and dad drank away most of their money and the time they weren't working. Like clockwork they'd be drunk by the evening and start jawing on each other, then pushing and slapping each other or him if he was around. His dad managed to keep his job only because he worked for his brother, who pitied his nephew for the parents he had drawn.

That uncle had been his savior, treating Golding like the son he'd never had and teaching him the business, including the underworld of fencing stolen property. Like his parents, Golding was irreligious and though he loved to gamble he didn't drink. His business was his life. Like his uncle, he had never married and always talked about women as whores and bitches.

His uncle frequented prostitutes and had taken Frank to his first house of ill repute in Reno when he was sixteen. His family liked to complain about how they hated the way the negroes were taking over their North Sacramento neighborhood and while his folks couldn't afford to move out, his uncle had built a walled complex and residence on his business lot and Golding had moved in when the uncle passed.

When the deaf bum left his building the first time he

had quickly called Maurice "the beast" Green with whom he had a long and profitable relationship. Green was a gangster, and a dangerous one at that. He laundered some of Green's dirty money through his official business and they were partners in crime. He sometimes called Green when he saw an opportunity to make money, but didn't want to get his hands dirty.

Golding had told Green about the homeless bum who was leaving his building with several thousand bucks in his pocket, but he had to call again after the bum came back to send most of his money home to Kansas. Still, Golding would get 40% of whatever Green's thugs could rob. He mostly trusted Maurice to give him his share since he knew how much money was involved. Green needed him to keep the money flowing between their partnership.

Maurice called him later that day to say his men had grabbed the guy and forced him to take them to his camp where they got $1,200, so he'd be including an extra $480.00 in the cash he'd be sending Golding at the end of the week.

Golding jumped in, "Hey, he should have had another $500 or so. He might have held out on them or they might have held out on you."

"Well, well, I'll check with my guys again."

"Did they ask him where he got the gold and if he had more?"

"Yeah they asked him and said he's harder than shit to understand. They said the guy can barely talk, but he swears he robbed a house and that was all the gold he had. They believed him, but if he shows up with more gold to sell you'll call me right?"

"Sure will, good doing business with you."

Tuesday afternoon Maurice called again. "I got some info for you about this homeless guy who had the gold," he began. "Last night one of our dealers talked to the deaf guy's buddy. I guess they camp together. The dealer said he got the camper fucked up and the guy told him that his buddy found gold in a tree, a lot of it, but he'd only brought back a couple pieces to cash in. He swore he'd held the two nuggets in his own hands. The dealer pushed him for info, and he said it was in an old tree near Paradise Beach, but he either didn't know anything more or wasn't saying."

"Son of a bitch!" Golding swore. "You know the gold

rush legend about a 49er hiding his gold in an old tree down by the river?"

"What? What the fuck you talkin' about." Golding rushed through the legend about the tree. "Sounds like crazy bullshit to me Frank," said Green.

Golding started to worry about the deaf guy going back for the rest of the gold. "If it's at Paradise Beach I may be able to find it," he said. "Look, when the guy came in my business and I saw he was deaf and could barely talk I only paid him half what the gold was worth and he took it without any question. I'll offer the five grand I made from the dumbass to you to shut him up and keep him from getting the rest of the gold."

"You want me to shut the motherfucker up for good? Shit he can barely talk as it is." Green laughed his deep, wicked laugh at his own joke. "If you mean what I think you mean it will take more than you're shitty five grand."

"For a fucking homeless guy?"

"Hell yeah, the cops will still get involved." After a pause he said, "You there man?"

Golding replied, "Let me think about this some more, maybe I can get to it before he does. Your guys roughed him up pretty good I guess eh, so he might be laying low. I'll get back to you soon on this."

He was glad Maurice thought the legend was bullshit. He couldn't believe his luck to have stumbled onto this guy. He thought, *Could a damn bum have finally found the gold? It sort of makes sense, hell they live in the fucking parkway. Shit! There are a lot of trees at Paradise Beach, but how many could be over one hundred fifty years old and bent? Maybe I should leave the office and head over there to look at trees.*

A few minutes later he thought, *This guy knows where the tree is and his buddy might too. What if they tell other people?* Golding called Green back and said, "Can you send over your two guys who robbed the deaf bum? I'd like to ask them some questions. Can they take me to your dealer, the one who heard about the gold?"

"You really serious about this gold treasure story huh? Okay, but we partners right? If you find it we'll do our usual forty/sixty split, right?"

"Fifty/fifty and we got a deal," he quickly countered.

"We'll see how much dirty work we got to do on this. How much gold are you talking about?"

"It could be between 100K and 200K."

Maurice whistled through the phone.

Golding had known and done business with Green for over ten years and knew quite a bit about his operation. Green led a gang of about 8-10 lieutenants who in turn handled all his drug dealing, each member selling to and collecting from scores of smaller time dealers. Green carefully insulated himself from handling much of the drugs and cash. He and his younger brother handled the big buys from the cartels or biker gangs and must have had piles of cash locked and hidden in secret locations. He always had a couple of his lieutenants in jail or prison and he bragged about taking care of his people. He'd once told Golding that he even helped the families of his folks if they got busted, which is why no one ever turned over on him.

He had also heard that Green had dirty cops and prison staff on his payroll. His tentacles reached into very dark corners of the underworld. His younger brother was his attorney. He'd sent him to law school and his brother defended his boys and helped him with the money operations. If he thought one of his people was disloyal or was stealing from him, they could disappear and so had his rivals in the drug trade. He was not called "the beast" for nothing. He was a very careful, shrewd and merciless operator who'd been arrested, but never charged with anything that stuck.

The more Golding thought about a stinking homeless bum getting the gold the angrier he got. *I deserve to get it, I've looked for it for fifty years and I'll be damned if this troll who can't even talk will walk away with my treasure. Even if I have to split it with Maurice, I could sell my business and walk away with a handsome retirement. Even if I can't find it, I can't let the bum get it, no fucking way!*

Chapter Seven - Battle for Gold

Saturday, April 13, 2002

Sam watched in his mirror as the black Honda slowly passed the driveway of the police station parking lot and continued on its way. Mota and Cat felt pretty uncomfortable, but agreed to go inside the station with Sam. They were lucky to catch Captain Ortega in the office on a Saturday. They filled Ortega in on the black Honda that had followed them from the hospital, the New Life resident who identified the car as one of the Beastie's, and the fact that Charlie had mentioned that some gang guys in a black Honda had grabbed Paul and robbed him at their camp the day he cashed the gold.

"Did you get the license plate on the Honda?"

They all shook their heads no. "Sorry, we blew that," said Sam.

Ortega immediately asked his staff to send a radio message to nearby patrol cars to look for the black Honda. He shared with them that his lieutenant had already been over to question Charlie who was cooperating and Charlie had remembered that Paul told him they wore yellow bandanas.

"I talked to my gang specialist and he said the yellow bandanas are worn by a South Sac gang, not the Beasties, but let me call him again." He called and spoke briefly with the gang task force leader.

"My guy says the heavily tinted black Honda sounds like a gang vehicle, and that the Beasties aren't into colors, but they have been known to wear the colors of other gangs to throw people off. You said this resident was with the Beasties and he was sure these guys were in the gang? And he's just out of prison?" asked Ortega.

"Yeah, that's what I understand. He was sure enough that he was pretty freaked out," replied Sam.

"Well, well, if our old friends the Beasties are involved then this investigation has moved to a whole new level. These guys are very dangerous and the head guy, Maurice Green, has been on our radar for many years as a suspected kingpin, murderer, and whatnot but we've never been able to bust him. We've busted a number of his boys, but they never give him up. Maurice's nickname is 'the Beast.' If they're following you, you are in danger. Charlie is in danger and the guy at New Life is very much in danger, because they don't let you leave the gang. We'd love to talk to the ex-Beastie guy."

Sam was quick to point out, "We didn't even see the guy. All residents at New Life are sworn to confidentiality. This guy's in the early stages of recovery and he's about to book out of there, so I'm reluctant to take the police to him. But I'll tell you what: we're close to his roommate and I'll ask him to broach the subject, though this guy might be as spooked by the cops as by the Beasties."

"Please do that," said Ortega. "If he knows as much as we would hope he does and if he's willing to give up Maurice Green then we could offer him immunity and refer him to the witness protection program."

Sam asked, "How does this gang get caught up with Tinker the same day he cashes gold in?"

Ortega nodded. "That's a good question. We were just looking at the gold cashing places that were within bicycle range of the campers and it's most likely the place on Northgate Boulevard. It's been around a long time and is owned by a guy who is a legit businessman, but we've heard talk of him fencing stolen goods. There might be a connection, but maybe the gang just got lucky. Maybe one of them saw Paul cash in the gold and figured he was an easy target."

"If these guys are keeping track of Charlie and following me then they must still be looking for the gold Paul found," Sam said, thinking out loud. "I'm glad Sheila went to the Bay area for the night, these guys might be able to figure out where I live."

"We were just talking on the way over here," added Mota, "and Cat and I think Charlie went to see this guy we know called Druggie Dave. He may have told Dave about the tree and the gold the night Paul cashed the nuggets. Druggie Dave might have ties to this gang. We don't know his last name do we?" He looked at Cat for help.

"I'm not sure," said Cat, "but I think his partner Jan's last name is Brown. Maybe they're married."

Captain Ortega wrote the name on his pad, nodded and said, "Well the gang was already onto Paul right after he cashed the gold, but maybe the information about the tree didn't get out until Charlie told this guy later that night and he told his Beastie contact the next day. If they were afraid Paul would go back and get the rest of the gold, they have motive to stop him Tuesday night or rather Wednesday morning."

Sam was weighing all this information and the fact that he could now be in danger and made a quick decision. "I might know where this tree is, where the gold could be hidden," he blurted. He glanced at Mota and Cat, then turned to Ortega. "I haven't told these guys about the tree being at Paradise Beach. It's probably a long shot, but I live by Paradise Beach and know it really well. Given what Charlie told me, I have a tree in mind. An old bent tree with branches like the fingers of a hand." Everyone looked at him in surprise.

"Look, this gold is not worth getting anyone else killed over, but it seems like a number of us are in danger now until it's discovered again," said Sam. "I'm thinking even if I don't have the right tree we may be able to lure the bad guys to it. The tree is at least close to the levee and easy to find. What if Mota and Cat pass the word to Dave the drug dealer that I know where the tree is and I'm putting together a team with metal detectors to get the gold tomorrow? You guys could tell him the tree is close to the levee at the Glen Hall Park river access point, which might get them to show up at Paradise tonight where you could grab them." He was nodding at Captain Garcia this time.

"I don't like using anyone as bait. If they can't find it they may decide to take you out and luring them out into a public place might endanger innocent bystanders at Paradise Beach," cautioned Ortega. "The other thing is that it's not illegal to look at trees in the Parkway, so we can't arrest them for that, but we can detain them for questioning and maybe we'll find drugs or weapons on them."

Sam countered, "Captain, they may already be over at Paradise Beach looking for the gold and if anyone sees them or gets in their way, it's already a risky situation. The beach closes at sundown so there shouldn't be many people there."

"Well, I might be able to put you under police protection for 24 hours and get a plainclothes detective at Paradise tonight to see what happens. I don't deny we've wanted Maurice Green for a long time. I need to run this up the chain of command here, but I think it's worth consideration. Can you guys hang out for a while longer?" They nodded and Garcia got up and left the room.

Sam got on his Village mobile phone and called

Sheila's sister in Oakland. No one answered, so he left a message that Sheila should definitely stay the night there as planned and it was important that she call him before she came home.

Then he called his friend and neighbor Mike McGill who was an anthropology professor at Sacramento State. "Hey, Mike, it's Sam. This is gonna sound weird, but bear with me. Have you heard the legend of the forty-niner lost gold hidden in a tree?" He listened, "Good, do you want to help me find it?" He arranged a meeting with him later that afternoon. Mota and Cat were getting restless and talked in lowered voices while he was on the phone.

"What's up?" Sam asked after he had hung up.

"We like your idea. We're just antsy to get going to the island and hope we can catch Dave," Mota replied.

The Captain came back in less than 15 minutes and said, "First of all, one of our patrol cars found the black Honda, but the guys had split with any damning evidence. The good news is that we've confirmed it is a vehicle known to be used by the Beasties. The chief is working on expanding the gang task force. If we can get the informer to work with us it would be huge.

"We should get help from our vice squad for an undercover officer to go to the tree at Paradise tonight and there will be protection for Charlie and your place tonight, Sam. I'm just not sure when we can get our plainclothes officer to the tree. It might not be until eight o'clock."

Sam looked at Mota and Cat, "I can give you a cell phone, so you can call me once you've found Dave. The guys in the Honda saw you two as well, so you may be in danger. Call the police if you run into the Beasties."

"They won't be able to find our camp anytime soon, but I'm thinking Cat and I should also go hide out by the tree until the plainclothes officer gets there. I'll use the phone to call you Sam, if the Beasties show up early. We'll just lay low." Sam then drew them all a map to where the tree was located.

Sam drove Mota and Cat west on the Garden Highway, past the five freeway and dropped them near the entrance to the island. "You guys be careful." He took an extra mobile phone from the Village that he kept as a backup in his truck and handed it to Mota. "Let me know how it goes with Druggie Dave." He showed them how to find his programmed number. "Take care, and I hope this will all be over by tomorrow."

———————————

Cat and Mota crossed the muddy inlet to the Island on their bikes and found Dave who seemed to be packing up with no sign of Jan around. The pit bull barked, but was tied up and Dave was sweating as he stuffed some of his junk into a large black duffle bag.

"Hey Dave!" they yelled as they approached and he jumped a bit.

"Looks like you're moving camp. Where's Jan? Can you hook us up real quick and we'll be on our way?" asked Cat.

"Yeah I can do that," Dave replied looking more haggard than usual. "Jan got locked up you know, we were in town getting supplies and she freaked out in the store, started screaming and throwing shit. I'm trying to get her out."

They did their business and Cat said, "Remember when you told us about Tinker finding a stash? Well, don't tell anyone, but we just found out from Sam White that it's true. Sam talked to Charlie today and Charlie told him about some gold Paul found in a tree and even where the tree is. Sam's planning to try to find it tomorrow morning."

"Do you know where the tree is?" Dave asked excitedly.

"Not exactly, but Sam said it's the biggest tree you see dead ahead when you come over the levee at Glen Hall Park." Cat had set the bait.

Dave watched the two customers turn the corner on the trail. He dug out his cell phone and made two calls, the first to his dealer to sell his information for a hundred bucks off his debt and another to his new benefactor.

"That's it I'm outta here, fuck this place." He was headed to some small town farther north up the five freeway where he could buy a trailer or rent something cheap by the Sacramento River and lay low. He was running with a good amount of crystal even though he still owed his dealer, which was dangerous, he knew.

"Fuck those assholes too," he said out loud as he threw the last of his crap in the second duffle. He thought about his wife Jan in the looney bin and yelled, "Good riddance!" He then walked away from his camp, a large duffel in each hand and his dog Lucky by his side. He left behind a huge mess of trash, bicycle parts, and a plastic bag of used needles.

After their visit to Dave, Mota and Cat had walked their bikes down the trail out of sight, but stopped to hear Dave talking to someone on his phone. They could only make out a few words of what he said, but they high fived each other.

"Mission accomplished!" Mota exclaimed.

They pedalled slowly and started discussing what to do next.

"You know these Beastie fuckers are going to be out looking for this tree and they're likely to get over there early, so we should too." said Cat.

"Yeah," replied Mota. "I know a way we could arm a small posse and head over there ourselves to keep an eye on Paul's tree. I'll ride to Evangeline's to buy supplies and you head back to camp and see if you can round up a posse. Tell them we're going after the guys who killed Paul and shot Charlie. I'll meet you back at camp in an hour or two."

Mota rode down the Garden Highway to Jibboom Street. He pedaled on the steep levee of the Sacramento River, which ran brown and high. Old Town was a tourist attraction with lots of bars, restaurants, art galleries, candy, and ice cream shops. Evangeline's was a one of a kind store with costumes and crazy tourist gizmos of all kinds, like fake dog shit. Mota remembered he had seen metal sling shots there, which were legal but serious weapons. He dug deep into his monthly disability check and paid almost one hundred and fifty dollars for eight of them and some cheap camouflage rain ponchos.

Mota rode into camp loaded down and Cat was already gathered there with Bandana, Gremlin and Jaws, Pit bull, Lizard, China, and Jube. Pit Bull and Lizard were moderately drunk, but were veterans you wanted on your side in a fight. Cat's friends China and Jube and Gremlin were the only sober ones. Gremlin always looked serious and Bandana—who was usually a jokester—appeared grim.

Mota shook hands all around and Cat said, "Everyone volunteered when I asked who wanted to find Tinker's killers and kick their ass. We all have bikes."

The drinkers passed around a small bottle of cheap vodka and Mota said, "Thanks for volunteering you guys. You may have heard the rumors that Paul found a stash. Well, this morning Charlie told Sam White that Tinker found a stash of gold hidden in a tree. Sam says he might know which tree. The trouble is a gang called the Beasties is involved."

Nobody seemed to recognize the name.

"They probably killed Paul and want to find his gold. These guys might already be looking for the tree, which is at Paradise Beach. We've set a trap for tonight by getting word to them about which tree it is, but we don't really know the gold is there. We think Druggie Dave probably deals with this gang and may have given up Tinker and Charlie. There will be a cop there at some point tonight, but I say we ride there soon and guard the tree until the cop shows up or until Sam can look for the gold. I'm not going to bullshit you, these guys probably have guns, but I did get us some weapons."

He reached into the sack he'd brought from Old Town and passed out sleek sling shots made of aluminum, rubber surgical tubing and leather.

As everyone handled their new weapons Cat chimed in. "Like Mota said, this could be dangerous and these are serious weapons we may need to use, so if anyone wants to bow out now is the time, no judgement, no problem."

She looked at every person eye to eye and they either nodded or said, "I'm in."

Cat nodded back with pride and said, "Okay then, I

guess we're the Odd Squad." Everyone cracked up at this name.

Bandana said, "I like it. I like it."

Lizard stammered, "F-f-fuckin A! R-right on!"

Jube, who was into a very religious recovery, said, "How about the God Squad?" Gremlin nodded okay, but everyone else wanted to stick with the Odd Squad.

They practiced for a while with the sling shots. Everyone was somewhat proficient and knew which size and shape of rocks worked best. They could sling a rock the size of a peach pit over fifty yards with some degree of accuracy.

Pit bull asked, "Why don't we just find the gold before they do?"

Mota replied, "Sam's not sure it's the right tree and he and Charlie are the only ones who know what part of the tree the gold is stashed in. Besides, we'd need a metal detector that we don't have and we want to lure these Beastie assholes who killed Paul to the tree. The plainclothes cop will come later tonight and if one or two of the gangsters show up he'll detain them for questioning. We might not need to do anything, they may not show up."

They all nodded agreement and together in a bike caravan they rode the foot bridge over the river and then east along the south levee. They arrived at Paradise Beach at sunset and found the tree.

Sam was breathing a bit easier now that Sheila had called him back—and though confused about how fast things were happening, she agreed to stay away from their house until late Sunday night. She was worried and tempted to come back earlier and stay with friends, but Sam downplayed the danger he might be in and emphasized the fact that he was promised police protection.

Sam next called Jake at New Life and asked him what he thought about approaching his roommate to cooperate with the police.

"Let me go outside real quick," whispered Jake stepping out his door. "I don't know Sam, he's been pacing and looking out the windows every fifteen minutes since he saw those guys."

"But if he has something on these Beasties he could get police protection and even enter a witness protection program and start over somewhere safe."

Jake hesitated a few moments, then said, "Look Sam,

I'll wait until after the meeting tonight, when hopefully he'll have relaxed a little and I'll see what he thinks."

"Thanks Jake, I know this is stressful for both of you at a time when you don't need it, but it could be very important."

Next Sam met with his buddy Mike McGill at the Tupelo coffee shop. Mike was on the edge of his seat, his hands clenched tight and his eyes wide, as Sam described what had happened over the past five days.

When Sam mentioned where he thought the tree was, Mike about jumped out of his chair and blurted at Sam, "You are shitting me!" About ten people in the coffee shop turned to look at them.

"Keep it down, Mike!"

"Sorry." Sitting back down Mike whispered, "We've been by that tree hundreds of times."

Sam was shaking his head. "I know, I know, but I could be wrong because I haven't had a chance to look yet."

"We've got to go right now. This is an anthropologist's dream!" Mike was on his feet again.

Sam got up and as they walked out the door he leaned in close to Mike's ear and whispered, "Did you not hear the part about the dangerous gang of drug dealers who were following me earlier today and the people they probably shot and killed? I want to go over there right now and look too, believe me, but we should wait until dark. I'm supposed to meet my police protection at the house in thirty minutes, can you come by and bring whatever equipment you think we'll need to look for the gold? You're the expert. We also need to figure out a plan for what to do if we actually find the gold."

"Sure," replied Mike. "I'll do a little research on the gold legend, I've seen references to it in gold rush era publications and follow up stories."

Later they were sitting at Sam's dining table where Mike's metal detector was on display. The realization that they could actually *find* the gold was starting to settle in—and now they had to decide what to do with it.

Mike was pumped up. "You realize what an amazing historical find this could be if it's the gold in the legend. Did you know the miner who stashed it was killed in the Squatter's Riots in 1850? We should package this for the media, it's a fantastic story!"

"Whoa, we need to be sure it's there before we talk to any media," Sam replied. "Mike, I want credit for this find to go to Paul and any financial gain should go to his family."

"Can we just give it to them?"

Sam cursed. "A horrible thought just came to me: there are probably legal ownership issues about the tree being in county parkland or the 49er's surviving family could make a claim. Maybe we'll need some legal advice."

There was a knock at the front door. Sam peeked through the window to make sure that it was an officer in uniform before he opened the door. Once the officer was inside, Sam introduced himself and Mike to the officer, Dave Romano.

Romano said, "I'll be watching the house until about 1:00 AM when the next shift will come on. Captain Ortega asked me to let you know that they can't get a vice squad detective down to the beach until after eight tonight." The officer gave Sam his phone number and said he'd be parked at the curb in front of Sam's house.

———————————————————

Cat and Mota sat down with the Odd Squad around the ancient twisted tree in the bottom of a sandy depression that stretched a hundred yards to the deep sand slope of Paradise Beach.

Mota said, "We need to be within range of the tree, but well hidden." They all looked around and saw only one option. On the North side of the tree away from the levee there was a ridge with a line of large trees and dense brush. Between the ridge and the tree was thirty yards of sand and rocks.

"Let's stash our bikes in the forest behind the ridge in the vines," suggested Cat, and everyone nodded.

Their bikes secured and well hidden, they moved out along the ridge and Mota passed out camouflage ponchos. Pit Bull and Lizard were closest to the tree and began to hollow out a spot behind some fallen branches covered in vines.

Pit bull growled, "This is fuckin' great cover."

Lizard agreed, "We c-can k-kick some ass from here."

Mota suggested, "Let's spread out along this ridge— maybe twenty feet apart." Gremlin and Bandana dug in behind a small brush covered wall of rock and sand. Mota found a small gap between two large trees in the middle. Cat decided she'd stay with China and Jube, so Mota helped them dig into the east end of the ridge.

The sun was sinking behind the tall cottonwood trees across the river and the three veterans began talking strategy.

Pit bull rasped, "They could charge our position with guns blasting, but they have to cross this clearing and we could fuck them over."

"Yeah, w-w-we'll f-f-uck them over g-good," Lizard said smiling.

"Depends on how many they are and how well armed," added Mota.

Pit bull said "They'll probably only have hand guns and their only cover is behind the tree. We'll surprise the shit out of 'em. I like our chances."

Mota looked seriously at the three women. "If they come after us you three need to retreat down the back of the ridge into the forest toward the river. It's only about fifty yards behind us and worst case scenario, you jump into the river and float downstream."

Cat shivered at the thought of jumping into the cold river at night. "We're not going to leave you guys behind." Cat shook her head.

"We'll cover you for as long as we can, then we'll be right behind you."

They agreed on a bird call that would signal the bad guys were here and another that would mean sling your rocks. They took some practice shots at the tree to get the range. Each collected a large pile of rounded river stones. Then they settled in for what could be a long night of waiting.

━━━━━━━━━━━━━━━━━━━

Sam and Mike waited until it was almost dark. There was a half-moon that peeked in and out from behind cotton clouds and the spring air smelled of roses and jasmine. They were armed with water, headlamps, a folded camp shovel, gloves, some climbing rope, a camera, and a rock hammer in day packs on their backs. Mike would carry the metal detector by hand.

Both men were deathly quiet as they snuck away. They didn't want Officer Romano to know they were leaving because Sam didn't want the Beasties to sneak in the house while they were out. They could call Romano if they needed back up. They climbed the back fence with a ladder and walked through the back neighbor's yard; Sam knew they were out of town for the weekend. They stayed off Carlson Boulevard and took the side streets to the river access at Glen Hall Park.

The public parking lot closed at sunset, but they noticed a black king cab truck with tinted windows parked across the street from the park. It looked empty.

Sam whispered, "This could be trouble, they might have beat us to the tree. Shit, these guys are not fucking around. I thought they might come tonight, but I didn't expect them so early and the vice cop isn't going to be here for an hour."

There were a couple other older cars parked across the street from the park, but they didn't look as suspicious.

Sam added, "Looks like we may have some other folks out here too, probably college kids partying." Mike nodded and pointed to the east end of the park away from the streetlights and toward a line of towering pine trees. They headed in that direction, staying in the shadows as they worked their way toward the levee.

It was just about dark when Cat and the others heard arguing and saw a group of four men dressed mostly in black come over the levee. The moon escaped from the clouds and they got a good look at the men. Three were younger and darker skinned. One was an older white man whose movements were stiff.

The older man didn't fit the description of a gang

member, but the others did. One of the young men was black and big with broad shoulders and long arms. The other two were small and wiry. Cat observed that one of the smaller guys seemed to be arguing with the older man, who pointed toward the tree.

The tree was between the Odd Squad and the supposed gangsters. Cat watched as the men walked toward the tree. She whistled the warning bird call and heard a couple of other folks return the call. The men were carrying shovels and what looked like a metal detector. When they made it to the old twisted tree the older man pointed to the exposed roots at the base of the bent over trunk. The younger men passed a joint and a flask around, getting in the mood to dig.

Mota crouched low and moved slowly behind the line of campers. He whispered in turn to each one, "We'll let them dig for a while, but if they find something I'll give the call to sling away."

The Odd Squad was dug in wearing the camouflage ponchos, waiting for Mota's call. Bandana and Gremlin smiled wickedly in anticipation.

Bandana whispered, "Let's do this for Tinker and Charlie" and Gremlin nodded.

The two older vets looked at Mota with bloodshot eyes and Lizard in a low voice said, "We'll m-m-make these s-s-sombitches p-p-pay!"

The women looked nervous but determined. Jube, lips moving without sound, prayed fervently. *At least her religious conversion hadn't ruled out revenge,* thought Mota as he squeezed Cat's hand. She smiled bravely and he returned to his spot. He called Sam on the phone, but it went to voice mail, so he left a quick message that the beasties had arrived as planned.

There was a small group about two hundred yards down river at the main sandy beach hooting around a fire. Mota heard a coyote call, the faint drone of air traffic, and the 80 Freeway. Otherwise it was quiet and they could hear the men argue among themselves about who should do the digging.

Every once in a while one of the men would complain. They'd say "What a load of shit this is," or "Ain't this a bitch?" before continuing their dirty work.

The old guy was holding the metal detector and moving the bottom end over the roots of the tree. They could hear it ping slightly when it went over one area, so two of the men dug in that spot. They found some old rusty metal object that was tossed away amid another round of complaints. They continued and each ping ended with disappointment and more cussing.

The older man started to shine his flashlight into the higher branches as he walked around the sizable girth of the tree, moving the metal detector back and forth, but found nothing. Then he climbed up onto the almost horizontal trunk and passed the detector over the base of the five main branches, nothing. He kept working his way up and when he ran the detector over the middle branch up as far as he could reach.

There was a loud ping.

Sam and Mike crouched over the top of the levee about fifty yards east of the main access road. They saw men digging around the tree with shovels. Sam saw that Mota had called and whispered to Mike, "Mota and Cat, the homeless folks I told you about are out here somewhere." Mike nodded as they scanned the area looking for some sign of them.

"Well they found the tree alright," whispered Sam. The levee afforded a clear view of the tree and the area around it. "They're digging around the roots, so they haven't found it yet. The gold's in the higher branches. Advantage to us."

They watched as the digging ended and the older guy started running the detector over the trunk and then the bottom of the main branches.

"Shit, they're moving their way up the tree, this is not good," whispered Sam. Soon after this they saw the same guy up in the tree reaching with the detector high up the middle branch. They heard a loud ping, then a strange bird call, and suddenly there was a commotion around the tree.

———————

After Mota heard the ping, his heart began to pound and he thought, *This is it!* He whistled the call to fire. Within seconds a barrage of rocks flew through the air toward the group around the tree. Rocks clumped against the tree or the ground.

At first the men looked around and at each other in confusion. Then a few rocks hit their marks and the men began to cuss and duck their heads. The older man was the most vulnerable up on the bent trunk. He fell awkwardly under the onslaught of flying stones, dropped the metal detector and bounced off the trunk, groaning as he hit the ground.

Another barrage hit the men and they dove for cover. One took a rock to the head and his hand went to his ear. He moved slower than the others and paid the price when the next volley landed.

The old guy was screaming, "Shit! My leg! My leg!" He crawled behind a twisted root and lay still.

The Odd Squad heard the men shouting, "What the fuck! Somebody's throwing rocks. Where are they?" The men soon figured out the rocks were coming from the direction of the ridge as more stones rained down on their position. They heard the faint sounds of slingshot tubing slapping as stones were catapulted, but they weren't sure what was making this noise.

Sam and Mike watched in awe as the guy with the metal detector fell with a thwack on the trunk, then hit the ground. Stones slapped against rocks and the tree as men continued to yell, cussing and digging in behind the tree roots.

After about a minute, Sam and Mike heard a shot and instinctively hit the ground on their bellies. Five or six more shots popped in quick succession and they could see smoke rising from around the tree.

Someone yelled, "Stop shooting you fuck heads!" and the shots ended. A deep silence stretched out over the park. Sam whipped out his cell phone and called Officer Romano.

When Romano answered Sam blurted, "This is Sam White and I'm at the river levee by Glen Hall Park. Shots have been fired!"

"I thought you were in your house," Romano hissed. "Has anyone been hit?"

"I don't know, we're okay so far, but hurry before the gangsters take off."

"I heard those shots. I'm calling for back up and on my way. How many shooters are there?"

"There's four guys and there had to be at least a couple guns." Sam added, "It's weird though. It looked like someone was throwing rocks at them before they fired."

The Odd Squad kept slinging at the men around the tree and had them pinned down. Then the men fired in their direction with pistols. The gunfire got their attention.

Mota ducked his head so fast his forehead bounced

off the sand and, heart pounding, he flashed back to hot dusty scenes of Desert Storm.

He blurted, "Incoming!"

Though it had been thirty years since their combat in Vietnam, Pit Bull and Lizard dove face first into the sand. Pit Bull's mind was invaded by visions of tropical forest exploding around them and men in jungle fatigues screaming. Lizard felt a rush of adrenaline pound in his head.

They all ducked for cover and waited out the volley of bullets, which fired wildly in their direction but only slammed into sand and trees.

There was a pause in the shooting as the echoes of gunshots bounced around.

Cat whispered to Jube and China, "Should we retreat?"

"Not unless they charge," China responded.

"Okay, let's wait to see what happens next." Cat peeked out at the gangsters.

It took several seconds that seemed to stretch into minutes, for Mota, Pit bull, and Lizard to gather themselves.

Mota whispered, "We've got to keep them pinned

down." They started slinging rocks again. Then the gangsters split up, with two moving away toward the levee and out of range. The other two headed toward their east flank. The campers could hear a siren close by.

Mota crawled quickly behind the line and told them to aim at the two headed toward their flank. The three women were closest to the two running men. They pelted them with river rocks and smiled triumphantly as the men yelped and tried to duck the onslaught. One of them fell hard and rolled, but popped up. Long before they could make it to the river the two men skidded to a stop and hid behind a cottonwood tree. They didn't fire back this time.

Jaws leapt over the ridge and bounded toward the two men behind the tree, barking and cutting off their escape to the river. When one of them lunged toward the river anyway, Jaws attacked, and the man screamed and tried to climb the tree with the beast clamped onto his lower leg.

In less than two minutes Romano screeched into the parking lot with red lights flashing and sirens squealing. Sam had seen the four guys by the tree split up; the big guy had lifted and dragged the older man, who limped badly. They struggled toward the levee, headed for the strip of Park behind the public pool complex. The other two guys ran east along the levee in Sam's direction, but then cut to their left on the trail that angled toward the river.

None of the men appeared to have guns in their hands. Sam and Mike hurried toward Romano who was still in his car in the parking lot apparently waiting for back up. They approached slowly waving their arms, so he could see who they were.

They warned him that the four shooters were wearing black and had split up, with two of them sneaking around him behind the pool complex toward the street. They looked up to see two police units racing down Carlson with sirens blaring and Romano got out of his car to direct his back up over the levee.

――――――――――

The two police cars came over the top of the levee and stopped to get the lay of the land below them. Their spotlights illuminated the two men in black.

One was hanging from a tree branch and the other was waving his arms over his head yelling, "Get this fucking dog off us!" Gremlin whistled for Jaws to return, which he did. Both cars slowly drove down the levee toward the men.

The officers jumped out of their cars with guns drawn yelling, "Get down on the ground!" The two men complied.

The victorious Odd Squad high fived and slapped each other's backs as quietly as they could manage while jogging down the backside of the ridge. They retreated through the forest toward their hidden bikes. They didn't want to get caught for starting the fight, so they buried their sling shots.

Cat whispered, "Those guys got more stoned than they planned on tonight." They all laughed and began digging in under trees and vines, their camouflage ponchos hiding them from the cops.

Soon a police helicopter arrived on the scene and searched the area with flood lights. After hearing the shots the college kids had put out their illegal fire and headed for the levee. The copter blasted a warning over loudspeakers that the parkway was closed and to disperse immediately. Soon the kids and the helicopter were gone.

Sam had pointed out the big black truck to Officer Romano. As they looked that way two guys came out from behind a tree in the park. The men in black moved across the street, the large one holding up the one who dragged his left leg.

Romano quickly swung his car around the end of the cul-de-sac and sped toward the truck, hitting it with his floodlight just as the big guy opened the driver-side door. Through his loudspeaker Romano told them to step away from the truck and lay down on the ground, which they did. He got out of his car, gun drawn, and approached them.

The two officers in the police cars that went over the levee had handcuffed the other two men, but didn't find any weapons. All five cops rendezvoused in the parking lot with Sam and Mike. The four suspected shooters were in the backseat of the two backup cop cars.

One of the backup cops reported, "We didn't find any weapons and they claim to be victims who were attacked by someone throwing rocks while they were just enjoying the night. They seem to have some serious wounds too. The old guy may have a broken ankle and one of the young guys has a nasty gash on his leg he says is a dog bite. They showed us a bunch of cuts and bruises they say are from stones that someone threw at them."

Sam jumped in, "We saw them fire at least a couple guns into the trees by the river, but we couldn't see who they were shooting at. It did look like someone was throwing rocks at them though." Sam then reminded Romano that these men were the murder suspects that he needed protection from.

Romano told the other cops, "I know it sounds crazy but I was briefed by Captain Ortega on the homeless murder and assigned to provide protection to this guy— who snuck out from under me without telling me he was leaving." He gave Sam a hard look.

"I'm really sorry," Sam said to Romano, looking contrite. "Look, their guns must be stashed down by the tree and if you call Captain Ortega, I'm pretty sure he wants to question these guys about the murder."

"We can hold them, but unless we find their weapons, it may be difficult to connect them to the murder. Regardless, they need some medical attention," said Romano. One of the officers called Ortega and confirmed that they were wanted for questioning.

Mike said confidently. "We can take you to their

weapons, we saw where they fired from and we have a metal detector that should make finding the guns fairly easy even in the dark."

With Romano watching, it took Mike only a few minutes to find two of the guns, which were just shoved under the sand by the tree's roots. A few more minutes led to a third gun about twenty feet away in some bushes. The officers could tell they'd been recently fired just by smelling them.

The officers took statements from Sam and Mike.

One of them told Romano, "We've got enough to charge these guys with discharging firearms in a public place, so they're on their way to the station after a stop in the emergency room. The helicopter didn't find anybody but kids partying on the beach, so we don't know who the rock throwers were or where they went."

After the two police cars left with the shooters, Sam approached Romano. "Mike and I need to find out for sure whether there's really gold in that tree and we'd like you to join us to be a witness and for our protection."

"I guess so, I'm on your protection detail for a few more hours, but just promise me you aren't going to try to lose me again," Romano said with a hurt look. The three of them walked back to the tree.

Mike turned on the metal detector and climbed up on the thick bent trunk headed for the middle branch. The metal detector pinged loudly. Mike climbed down to leave the metal detector and to grab his camera, and then he and Sam climbed up a bit farther with their head-lamps and daypacks to get a better look.

"I'll be damned," said Mike as he found a good sized hole that had been stuffed with bark and bits of small-er branches. They both climbed closer. Mike snapped photos, then they started to scrape away the debris from the hole. They quickly spied a metal box inside and yelled excitedly down to Romano that they'd found something.

"Put on gloves before you touch it! The victim may have left fingerprints—we can use those to prove he found it first!" Mike flashed more photos, and then they pulled on their gloves. As they extracted the heavy box they spotted another underneath just like it.

"Can you believe this?" Mike gasped and Sam just shook his head, speechless.

Mota, Cat, and the Odd Squad had come out of their holes and were again in the thick trees near the site of their battle, but they maintained a good distance and a quiet presence. When they heard Sam and his friend say they had found something, the campers could hardly believe their ears. The gold was real!

Bandana and Gremlin smiled so wide it looked like their faces might split in two. Mota and Cat were half-dancing on the grass, with hands clasped and shit-eating grins on their faces. China pumped her fists in the air, while Jube prayed with fervent gratitude, her eyes closed tight. Pit bull and Lizard just chuckled and took a pull off a vodka bottle they'd brought along. Even Jaws was excited—his dinosaur smile said, *Did you see me tear into that guy?*

They each felt a strong but unfamiliar pride swelling in their chests, as they savored the moment knowing they had done their job and saved Tinker's gold.

Sam and Mike were breathless as they sat on the bench of tree trunk and opened the first box. Mike shot photos rapidly. Sam gently pulled the piece of deer skin off the top and thought he saw faint writing etched on one side. He held it up for Mike to read:

PROPERTY OF MICHAEL O'CONNOR 1850

"This proves the legend," Mike said in a hushed tone, the historic implications washing over him. "This is big!"

They both turned the light from their headlamps to the box and it glinted off the gold nuggets.

"Mother of God!" exclaimed Romano when they tipped the box to show him. "I wouldn't believe it if I wasn't seeing it with my own two eyes." They opened the second box and saw more gold nuggets and vials of gold dust. Mike took photos of the two open boxes, then carefully closed them and climbed the rest of the way down. Sam and Mike hugged, their hearts racing. They both laughed like children and danced, hooting around the tree.

In the forest nearby the Odd Squad was rolling around in the grass and sand, choking back their own laughter. Some cried, tears flowing freely both for joy and sadness as they wished Tinker were here to see this. Mota's phone vibrated in his pocket and he saw it was Sam's number.

"Hey Sam," he whispered.

"Mota, I wanted to let you know right away that we just found the gold in the tree."

"I know," Mota smiled, "we're close by."

"Gotcha, we'll talk later." Sam hung up and when he was sure Romano wasn't watching he waved at the trees across the clearing.

Late Saturday night, Jake and his roommate Chico were in their small apartment at the New Life recovery program talking about that evening's meeting.

Jake decided now was the time to take a chance. "I know you're freaked about seeing your old gang today. I talked to Sam White a while after he left here. I trust him. He asked me to talk to you. After being followed by the guys you spotted, Sam met with a police captain, Ortega, who's on our friend's murder case. They think your old gang may be involved in Tinker's killing. Anyway, Sam happened to mention that my roommate recognized their car."

Chico's eyes opened wider and he focused on Jake's face. "Oh fuck me! You're kidding right? Tell me you're kidding."

Jake quickly added, "Sam doesn't even know your name and he refused to tell them where you are. Sam said the cops are willing to offer you a witness protection deal and immunity if you'd meet with them and give them info on these Beasties."

Chico stood up suddenly. "I know Maurice Green, to talk about him is a fucking death sentence. Shit! I just wanted to get clean and stay out of trouble, but trouble finds me every fucking time." He crumpled to the couch, his head between his knees like he was going to be sick.

After a minute he composed himself and looked back up at Jake. "I did two years in Folsom prison for that ass-hole. He ordered me to beat the shit out of another dealer and his brother arranged my plea bargain.

"He told me he knew where my mother lived in Oakland so I wouldn't rat on him. He sent her money when I got locked up, like that made everything okay. I was kidding myself to think I could come back into his neighborhood and stay away from him. He's fuckin' evil and he acts like he's your friend, but he's all about number one. I used to be close to him. I don't think he knows that my mom died right before I got out and I don't have any other family he can threaten me with, so it's just me. Maybe I should talk to the cops, but Maurice has people on the inside."

Jake promised Chico that he could trust Sam and Sam could set up a meet with Captain Ortega in any way that would make Chico feel safe.

"Safe is a joke when you're talking about Maurice 'the beast' Green," said Chico with a bitter laugh. "I know enough to fuck him over, but I've got to be under protection from the get go and it's got to be out of this town."

Jake said, "I'm sorry to spring this on you when you're doing so well in recovery, but maybe you can start fresh."

"Yeah, whatever. It's the only chance I've got now."

Jake called Sam right away. "Hey Sam, I just talked to Chico and he's agreed to have you set up a meeting with Captain Ortega. But he's afraid of this Green guy getting to him because Green has people on the inside. Are you sure you trust this Ortega? You need to keep Chico safe."

Sam without hesitation said, "I trust Ortega; he wants Green badly. I'll call Ortega right away. Thanks for doing this Jake! I'll try to make this happen as soon as possible." Sam then told Jake about setting the trap for the Beasties, how the gangsters actually located the gold with a metal detector, and then were driven off and arrested before they could get their hands on it.

"Some people from your old neighborhood beat them back by throwing rocks from behind trees." They both had a good laugh; Jake was pretty sure who Sam was talking about.

"What a crazy story," said Jake. "You actually have Paul's gold?"

"Well, we left it with the police, but there were two boxes of gold with the name of the guy who left it there in 1850. If there are no claims on it we're hoping it goes to Paul's family eventually." Sam thanked Jake again and said good night.

When Mota, Cat and the Odd Squad rode back to their camps they were still pumped from the rush of their victory, but that didn't last long. At their camp they were greeted by official notices from the Park Rangers pinned to their tents.

"You are camped illegally in a county park pursuant to Sacramento County Code #2000-B125," the notices read. "You have forty-eight hours to remove your belongings or they will be confiscated and this area will be cleaned of all debris."

"Not exactly a hero's welcome," sighed Mota.

"Motherfuckers!" Cat spat angrily.

They wouldn't let this pull them down, not tonight. Except for China, Jube, and Gremlin, the Odd Squad ingested the last of their drugs and alcohol. Battle stories were retold and they could not remember when they'd laughed this much or felt this good.

PART FOUR

Chapter Eight - In Tinker's Honor

Monday, April 15, 2002 - Sacramento State University Media Center

Cameras clicked and flashed as Sam and Mike held blown up pictures of Paul Dixon and the tree between them. They had just opened the two rusted boxes of gold on a table in front of the crowd with a flourish. Even the reporters had gasped in surprise.

All the local TV stations, the Sacramento Bee, and the main wire services were in attendance at the press conference organized by Carly Johnson in cooperation with Sac State. Kalen was there, and Sam had made sure the Odd Squad was in attendance too. Mota and Cat had told him the story of the slingshots and their battle. He would leave that part out.

Mike McGill spoke to the press first, explaining that Michael O'Connor had been a sailor from Boston, an Argonaut, and gold rush prospector who had mined the gold and stashed it into the tree. He showed the reporters the name burned on the strip of deer skin, still legible after 152 years. He explained that on August 14, 1850, O'Connor had died at the Squatter's Riot as a bystander before he could return for his treasure. Mike had done his homework on the legend of the gold and described how O'Connor had told Father Anderson, a Catholic priest, about his stash before he died, thus creating the legend of the gold hidden in a twisted tree along the river.

Mike finished, "Paul Dixon should be credited with this amazing historical discovery found less than a mile from where we are standing."

Sam then told the story of Paul Dixon, the homeless man who was much loved by his fellow campers and staff at the Village and who was severely hearing impaired. He spoke of how Paul found the gold the week before (his fingerprints on the boxes had been confirmed) and how he'd cashed two gold nuggets only to be discovered by local crooks who stole his money and probably took his life.

"Paul Dixon sent most of the money home to his deaf father in Kansas despite his own struggles. It is ironic that Paul Dixon and his campmate were victims, yet the city and county are treating the campers like criminals forcing them to move or citing and arresting them." Sam added, "Tomorrow we will begin an ongoing sit-in at the County Supervisors' lobby in Paul's honor and his memorial service will be held Wednesday morning at St. Francis Village."

Captain Ortega then made a statement that their investigation into Paul's murder had finally uncovered a motive and pointed to potential suspects, but that it was still too early to comment on the specifics of the case. He also refused to comment about the camping violations that the park rangers and police had issued.

The reporters, of course, launched into questions about who owned the treasure; the presenters all agreed that this was for the lawyers to resolve and might take some time. After the press conference, Sam and Mike led a press caravan to the site of the tree for a photo shoot.

The news story spread like windblown wildfire on parched plains, first across the country then internationally. The gold itself was valued at about one hundred and fifty-thousand dollars, but given the historic background and amazing story of being lost and then found by a homeless man, the collection was thought to be worth twice that.

The bad news was that none of the weapons found Saturday night near the tree matched the murder weapon. The four men in custody all had alibis for the night of the murder that had so far checked out. The police were going to have to release two of the suspects the next day. They were claiming self-defense in the firing of their weapons and couldn't be linked to the murder. Given the evidence that someone had thrown rocks and injured the four, their claim of self-defense was bolstered and the District Attorney was reluctant to press charges.

Two of the younger guys were on probation and should not have had weapons, so they would definitely remain in jail. Franklin Golding was recorded on security videos at a local card casino all night on the night of the murder, but he wasn't getting off scot-free. Captain Ortega had obtained a search warrant for Golding's business and the search earlier that day had uncovered the two gold nuggets and Paul's bill of sale. It looked like they might be able to charge him with embezzlement.

It was obvious that Golding was connected to the Beasties—and therefore Maurice Green. Ortega wanted to put the screws to him and his business. He had already talked to the FBI about investigating Golding for money laundering. Cosmo Green, Maurice's brother and lawyer, was representing Golding and the Beasties. Ortega was looking for Maurice to bring him in for questioning, but he was a slippery eel.

Even with everything they had uncovered, the police still had their work cut out for them. They had offered Golding a deal if he would roll over on Maurice Green, but so far he admitted to nothing. With Cosmo Green representing him, he wasn't likely to. Ortega had a meeting set with Chico the former Beastie later that day and hoped this would tighten the noose around Green and his organization.

———————————

Tuesday morning dawned bright, sun-spattered pine needles overhead as Sam sat with Sheila in their back yard. She looked at him grinning and shook her head; he smiled back and shrugged his shoulders.

Sheila had returned Sunday night. Monday morning she had a staff meeting, so she missed the press conference, but had seen the TV coverage. They could barely believe the sensation the gold had created and the notoriety that had befallen Sam. Media interview requests were still streaming in for him.

"All the times we've drummed and run by and even climbed that tree," Sam said shaking his head. "It seems like a dream now, but life goes on. Remember I may not be home tonight. Our sit-in starts today and we could be camping out. I hope all this hype about the gold will help today's news coverage of the sit-in and not be too much of a distraction."

"Yeah, good luck with that," said Sheila. "I'm sorry, I've got a meeting tonight so I won't be able to join you."

By nine o'clock that morning all the Village board members were sitting in the public lobby of the Sacramento County Supervisors. They had posters, graphs, and pictures illustrating the need for housing and shelter for homeless women and children. There was a photo of Tinker with a heading, "Don't punish the victims." County staff were busy ignoring them and no doubt in their back offices discussing whether they could have the protesters removed.

By noon they were joined by a dozen faith leaders representing Catholic and Protestant, Jewish, and Muslim communities. They held a press conference outside the second floor entrance. Sister Julie and Reverend Don took the lead, stated the demands of the sit-in and made the promise that advocates would be sitting in the Supervisor's lobby every weekday for as long as it took.

Sam refused to answer any questions about the gold except to say that they would hold the memorial service for Paul Dixon the following morning at ten AM at the memorial wall in Dignity Park. At two o'clock the staff of Dorothy Day House had transported thirty-six homeless women and children to attend the county supervisors' weekly meeting. They weren't on the agenda so they waited to give testimony. They wanted the five supervisors to have to look into the faces of the women and children they were refusing to help. Two of the five supervisors were in strong support of increased housing and shelter and admonished their three peers for not acting.

After the Supervisors' meeting Sister Julie approached Sam, who was still sitting in the lobby.

"It looks like we're going to have about forty women and kids with no place to go tonight," sighed Sister Julie. "I've asked them if they'd be willing to camp out here with our support and most have said yes."

"Okay," said Sam. "I'll kick the campout into gear."

Staff and board members were waiting for the word to send media notices and bring dinner later. Sister Julie had assured the women that they wouldn't be arrested. She and Sam had a backup plan in case they were threatened with arrest.

By five-thirty there were over twenty children of all ages and races, eight single moms, one couple, and ten single women accompanied by Sam, Julie, and three other Village staff members. Cat, Mota, Jube, and China joined them later.

Most people lounged on the small square of grass against the side of the county building. Sam was a veteran of homeless campouts on this site, so they had brought plastic buckets to use as seats and the Village truck was parked at the curb with a lift gate down and a porta potty in the back. A couple local TV station reporters and cameramen had already stopped by to get footage of the campout.

At six o'clock, Sister Julie noticed a young woman holding her infant and a single plastic bag cowering in a corner of the concrete shelf ringing the patio. Sister Julie didn't know her so she approached.

"I'm Sister Julie, welcome to the campout. We have

sleeping bags and people will be bringing food soon."

"Thank you so much, I'm Jane," the woman whispered, "I was sent here by the District Attorney's office after they figured out the battered women's shelter was full. They'll give me a bus voucher to leave town tomorrow, but my husband has threatened to kill us, so I can't be seen on TV or anything."

Sister Julie's face was etched in concern and she advised Jane, "TV cameras were here earlier and might return, so make sure and cover up when they're here. We'll do our best to keep you hidden."

The private security guards for the county came out after the building closed and told people they had to move off the patio, inciting fear among some of the campers. Sam and Sister Julie told the guards these women and children had no place else to go, so they'd be staying until the county offered an alternative.

A few minutes later they heard the sprinkler system activate. Sam sprang into action, telling folks to put the buckets over the sprinkler heads. The grass got wet fast, so they had to congregate on the concrete.

Then two city police cars rolled to a stop in front of the building and Sam turned to Julie. "Here we go."

A female police officer walked up the front stairs and was met at the top by Sam and Sister Julie.

"I'm Sergeant Meade," said the officer. "Are you representing this group?" Sam and Sister Julie nodded wordlessly. "The County Executive has sent me to ask you to move off their property."

Sister Julie was resolute. "You can see that we have mostly families with children who are homeless. Where does the County Executive expect them to go?"

"Look," said the officer whose head darted around counting the children. She was clearly not excited about her role. "If you refuse to move and they give us the order we'll be forced to arrest whoever stays."

"You do what you have to do and we'll do what we have to do," Sam said as they returned to their respective corners.

Sister Julie and Sam brought together all the adult campers and explained what the police had threatened.

"We expected something like this, so our plan is to leave if they really come to arrest us and walk over to City Hall across Ninth Street. Then if they pursue us we'll go back to the Village and everyone can stay at Day House."

Cat blurted, "They threatened us with their rent-a-cops, tried to spray us with sprinklers and now the police, fuck that!"

One of the mothers squared her jaw. "If they're going to arrest us for being homeless, let 'em try!"

Others yelled, "Yeah!" or nodded in anger.

"We promised that you and your children would be safe, so we plan to honor that, but let's push them as far as we can," said Sam, impressed with their courage.

A couple in their sixties came up the steps to join the campers. Sam approached them and introduced himself. The man only grunted, but shook Sam's hand so hard it hurt.

The woman said, "We are Paul Dixon's family and we've just arrived today from Kansas."

"Glad you could make it! It's an honor to meet you. I'm Sam White, the Village director. My coworkers and I arranged for you to come."

"Yes, we know," said the woman tearfully. "We saw the TV coverage of your campout—and in honor of Paul, too. Our motel is just around the corner, so we walked over." She was signing to Paul's father as she spoke and continued to act as translator.

Sam offered, "I'd like to introduce you to some of Paul's friends." He brought over Sister Julie and the Odd Squad.

Within ten minutes another five city police cars joined the other two in front of the building. Sam pulled out his phone and called one of the TV reporters who had come out earlier. He was sympathetic and had offered to return if the police came.

Sergeant Meade had been on her phone and now came back up the stairs. Again Sam and Sister Julie met her at the top, but this time an angry group of desperate mothers stood strong behind them.

"The county says you have to vacate their property or risk arrest."

"If the county wants to look like heartless fools we'll accommodate them," snapped Sister Julie.

The mothers echoed, "Where are we supposed to go?" Sam added that the parents of the murdered homeless man had joined them. He hoped other staff and board members would join them soon—and, more importantly, the press. Humanizing these homeless families was key to the Village's strategy.

Sergeant Meade now stood behind her car, having an

animated discussion on her phone, probably with some county official. This call seemed to go on for a long time. Sam and Sister Julie watched her tensely, not knowing how this was going to play out. Doors on the police cars began to open. The seven cop cars were quite a show of force, but most of the officers hadn't exited their cars to prepare for arrests and didn't seem anxious to do so.

Finally, the channel nine reporter and cameraman came around the corner and started climbing the stairs. As if on cue Sergeant Meade ended her phone call, got in her car and led the parade of cop cars down I Street until they turned a corner and disappeared.

Sam was shaking hands with the TV reporter saying, "You just saved our butts." Sister Julie was hugging some of the women and congratulating them on their courage.

The women smiled and high fived each other saying, "We showed the county," and "You can't scare us off that easy!"

By the time dinner arrived everyone was in a high mood and feeling empowered. Paul's family returned to their motel. The rest of the night went pretty smoothly, though sleeping on the cement was uncomfortable and humbling for the housed people.

Around nine that night Sam got a call from Captain Ortega. "Hey Sam, our meeting with Chico went really well. We've placed him in protective custody. Chico gave us a lot of inside information about the Beasties and some damning testimony against Maurice Green.

"Chico's been out of their loop for a while, so not everything will pan out, but we're excited to have some solid leads. We hope to find Green and some of his contraband real soon. Thanks again for setting this up. I just wish we had something more solid on Paul's murder, but don't worry we're still working it."

Chapter Nine - A Kind of Justice

Wednesday, April 17, 2002

Sister Julie and Sam led the protesting mothers and children back to the Village at eight in the morning, thanks to the Village's Homeschool program vans driven by its teachers. The women and children were now enjoying eggs and pancakes at the Day House dining room. Sheila had brought Sam a change of clothes. He had cleaned up and changed and was now meeting with Pastor Don.

Sam said, "Thanks for picking up Paul's father and stepmom at the airport and for putting them up close by. They're very sweet folks."

Pastor Don replied, "They really are. I updated them on what I know of Paul's case and they had already heard about the gold. I hadn't thought to invite them to the sit-in, but it was so great they came on their own. I went to see Charlie too and the doctor wouldn't release him to come today, they're afraid of infection and him moving around too much. It's just as well; I don't think he wanted to come anyway, he's still feeling guilty."

"Too bad, he'll be missed."

Close to ten that morning, hundreds of guests had gathered at the memorial wall in the back corner of Dignity Park. Water flowed over the rock wall, with over two hundred and fifty names of deceased homeless men and women chiseled onto dark marble in the center. Park staff had moved over as many benches as would fit and there was still standing room only. The media was asked to stay outside the park.

Paul's cart was front and center, holding his prize possessions: his makeshift collection of tools, wire and duct tape, his dictionary and frayed paperbacks and all the other things he never went anywhere without. Over the side lay a garland of spring flowers with a framed photo of him as a younger man balanced on top. Paul's father and stepmom sat in the front row. They were flanked by the Odd Squad, Jake, Sam, and Sister Julie. Behind them sat Batman and Robin in civilian clothes. Village staff and board members were sprinkled throughout the colorful crowd of men and women.

Pastor Don led the service first in prayer, then with personal witness. "We knew brother Paul Dixon, the Tinker, to be a kind man, quick to smile, always willing to help by fixing what was broken. It turns out that Paul also had a knack for finding long lost treasure. When he cashed in some of the lost gold he found, the first thing he did was to send most of the money to his father in Kansas." Don paused and Paul's stepmother finished translating in sign language to his father who nodded and smiled. "Unfortunately we know now that Paul's treasure, his ticket off the streets, attracted criminals who robbed and killed him.

"Today we remember Paul, and we pray for justice. We pray for Paul's good friend Charlie still recovering in the hospital from a grievous wound and for Paul's family who are with us today. We pray that Paul's life will not be forgotten, and we pray that his good will lives on in others. We pray that we can live our lives like Paul lived his—helping others. I'd like to have a moment of silence. We have lost a good man."

Pastor Don choked on his last words and tears flowed from many of those present. Sam's throat constricted and he cried without shame. He put his arms around the shoulders of the people on either side of him and this gesture spread throughout the crowd. People's arms entwined or they hugged or held the hand of the person next to them. There was a long healthy silence as everyone there joined in physical and loving contact with the whole, thinking of Paul and Charlie.

Then it was Sam's turn. He wiped his eyes with a handkerchief as he stood in front of the throng. "Thank you all for being here today to honor our friend Tinker, Paul Dixon, a kind, gregarious man. I mean, you knew when Paul was around right?"

Everyone chuckled. It was true; Paul had always been one to stand out from the crowd with his loud and irregular speech, quick to help others and friendly to all the campers.

"Paul loved to help others fix things," Sam continued. "All you have to do is look around us inside the park. The blinds he fixed on the windows inside the hutches where he loved to play backgammon. The many carts and bikes in those racks he fixed for free or for whatever folks could trade." Sam paused to let the lump in his throat subside.

"We've all had dreams of finding treasure or something valuable that would change our lives. Paul lived this dream, finding a long-lost stash of gold that had fostered a legend one hundred and fifty-years old. His powers of observation, keen eyesight, and curiosity led him to this treasure. The greed of gangsters quickly turned his dream into a nightmare. Where is fairness? Where is justice?"

"Well, we have here today scores of experts in un-fairness. Am I right?" The crowd murmured its acknowledgement. "Thanks to help from his friends"—Sam nodded at the Odd Squad who nodded back with proud smiles—"friends who put their lives on the line, his treasure and his memory have been protected for posterity. Here at the Village Paul will be long remembered as the kind and helpful "Tinker" who faced his challenges with dignity and compassion."

Jake stepped up next and brought Mota and Cat with him. "Paul and Charlie were our friends and camp brothers. They never hurt anyone. They didn't deserve to be shot by some coward while they slept. Paul finally had some good luck finding the gold and he's dead a few days later. It makes me wonder: is there a just God? And if there is why does she seem to hide when we need her? I swear, sometimes it feels like we're just monkeys howling in the wind. But this world is what we've got and friendship helps us survive it. We love you Paul!"

Over thirty folks followed Pastor Don, Sam, and Jake in giving their own witness, the crowd laughing and crying with the speakers. A few were quite drunk and could barely put a sentence together, but they were not judged too harshly by this crowd.

After the last speaker, Paul's father stood up and turned toward the throng. His bald head and weathered face showed all his sixty-five years but his body was as wiry and muscled as that of a twenty-five year old. His wife stood beside him to translate his sign language.

He simply said, "I'm proud of my son Paul, my only child. I knew him as a good boy, a hard worker, and I love him. I can see he touched many of you. Thank you for honoring his life." Tears slid down his cheeks as he sat back down and was enveloped in his wife's embrace.

Pastor Don and Sister Julie then led the crowd in singing Amazing Grace. Jake and Mota's eyes fixed on Cat in surprise as she belted out the tune with eyes closed, her voice strong and heartfelt. With that, the service was officially over. There was a slow dispersal with lots of hugging and supportive murmurs.

Paul's father and stepmom were invited to lunch in the main dining room and they graciously accepted.

After lunch Paul's stepmom translated his father's gratitude to scores of volunteers: "I want to thank you all for welcoming my son, helping to feed him, and giving him and so many others in need a safe place."

Jake had enjoyed being back at the Village after a week of seclusion at New Life. He had come to honor his friend Paul, though he definitely felt the strong pull of alcohol and friends. He fought back thoughts of heading to the nearest liquor store and hanging out with drinking buddies, so he went in to see Tony at the Living Sober office. Tony, as always, was encouraging and supportive. He knew well what Jake was feeling.

"I'm glad you came to honor Paul, but we've got to get you back to the program. You're thinking about your old friends and alcohol. Am I right?"

Jake shook his head reluctantly. "Does it ever get easier to not think about it? I mean I really don't want to go back to that life, but I can't get these thoughts out of my head."

"I know," said Tony. "It gets a little easier as time passes and you fill your life with positive people and things that make you happier, but there's a reason we say, 'One day at a time.' You're only a week in Jake, so don't be too hard on yourself. Just trust the program and you'll make it."

"Yeah, I know," said Jake, but he still wasn't entirely sure.

Tony kidded, "Hey, you sure got rid of your roommate fast. Really, though, I'm glad he's in a safe place. I encouraged him to get into a program fast wherever he ends up and he promised he would. If he can help get this Green guy put away then all the better. You did a good thing, Jake."

Jake nodded sheepishly. He was glad that everything with Chico had turned out for the best.

Then Tony remembered, "We have a new resident coming to the program today, someone you might know. I wondered if you could introduce her to folks and help her get settled in."

"Who's that?" asked Jake curiously.

"It's Jan Brown, you know Druggie Dave's ex-partner?"

"Yeah, I knew Dave and Jan a little bit, she was really out of it talking crazy shit all the time. She's really in recovery?"

"Yeah, she was in the county mental hospital and is going through meth withdrawals. She's still on meds, but they're releasing her this afternoon. She's at least tracking okay and saying the right things, so I said we'd give her a try. Apparently Dave has disappeared and abandoned her."

"I'm not surprised about Dave. Sure, I'll do my best to welcome her."

"Thanks, Jake. It's always a great help to have somebody you know welcome you. Come on, let's get back to New Life; I'll give you a ride."

———————————

Maurice Green sat on the edge of his chair in his brother Cosmo's law office on Del Paso Boulevard late Wednesday morning. Franklin Golding, left leg in a walking cast, and the big Beastie named Amos sat on a couch after being released that morning from the county jail. They had just told the Green brothers their story.

"You've fucked us Golding! Your gold treasure hunt has made the dead fucking homeless guy a hero and we're the chumps. I've lost two men and you even got your asses kicked by a bunch of ghosts with sling shots. Is that what you're telling me?" Maurice spat, veins bulging in his neck.

Golding blurted, "That was a trap, a set up. That guy White who claimed he found the gold knew we were coming and ambushed us. The gold was in that tree, I found it before they did!"

"It doesn't fucking matter when you're chased off like a bunch of pussies and the other guy grabs it." Maurice said, sneering at Amos and Golding.

Golding wanted to say, *You weren't complaining when you snatched twelve hundred bucks from the deaf guy I put you onto*, but he kept his mouth shut.

"So here's where we are now." Cosmo steered them to more urgent matters. "You guys know they're probably following you right? The pigs may be out there right now, but they don't know where Maurice is and we want to keep it that way. We've established everyone's alibis for the guy's murder, so I think we put that behind us.

"But the cops are all over your business now Franklin. I heard they might bring in the FBI on suspicion of laundering, which we've prepared for. In fact, I have a file cabinet full of invoices that will make sure we're covered. They are at the massage parlor and I need to get them to your office right away. You are more vulnerable on this embezzlement charge in the short term. I'll be talking with the DA about whether they plan to actually pursue it. With the vic dead they may not."

"Who'd you get to do it Franklin? I know you hired someone to shoot those fuckers because you offered me chump change to do it," said Maurice, still furious with Golding for bringing so much heat to his business.

"I have an airtight alibi and I'm not admitting to anything. You know they offered me a deal to turn on you and I told them to fuck themselves?"

"You better not be bullshitting me Golding, people who bullshit me have been known to disappear." Maurice's murderous eyes burned into Golding's, and Golding was the first to turn away. "I'm providing you free legal services so far Golding, but if this drags out you're going to owe me big."

Golding looked like he wanted to protest, but before he could, Maurice had waved him and Amos away. Golding knew he was on thin ice as it was; you didn't stay with Maurice Green any longer than you had to on a good day. He and Amos left without another word.

As soon as Maurice was alone with his brother he

asked, "So you think we can defend our laundry system if the feds investigate?"

"It depends on how deep they dig, but it would take them months. Obviously we'll have to stop Golding's piece. We don't want the heat to poke around in our other businesses."

Maurice thought for a minute, then gave his brother a knowing look. "I think if Golding disappears, so does his connection to us. He'll look like the guilty party who fled charges. I'll have my guy deliver your file cabinet to Golding. So call Golding and tell him the guy is coming today."

After finishing with his brother, Maurice opened the heavy lock on the door to the back room of his brother's office. The building was a fortress with all manner of alarms and defenses. He pulled out the bottom drawer of a large file cabinet. The file cabinet then rolled aside to reveal a narrow stairway that angled down into a cement tunnel.

Maurice squeezed into the tunnel, which broadened into a good-sized space that held a desk with a computer and some cell phones. There was a safe within a vault and after spinning the combinations Maurice took out twenty-thousand dollars in cash already stuffed into a money belt.

He called his contact. A message-machine beeped, "Leave your password, name, age, address and directions."

"This is the Prophetess of Love," said Maurice, and looking at his key code sheet Maurice spelled out Golding's name and address. "Pick up a file cabinet at 2201 Truxel and deliver it. Make it look like a run away with all valuables."

He hung up, then made a few other calls. After a while he continued underground to the end of the seventy-foot tunnel and up a steep spiral metal staircase. He pushed up a levered hatch at the top and stepped into a utility closet in his warehouse on an industrial lot behind his brother's office.

When he opened the door and entered his second-level offices he was greeted by an interagency SWAT team in black combat gear and helmets.

"Down on the floor, dirt bag!"

Maurice hesitated for only a second, until he saw at least three automatic weapons pointed at him.

He got down on his knees just as a big guy yelled,

"Down on your stomach!" and jumped on his back. He was truly shocked by the rude ambush and as they cuffed him roughly he thought, *that fucking Golding sold me out*!

One of the guys in black said, "Look what we got here," and held up the money belt.

They even knew about my tunnel, he thought, which he had never told Golding about—he hadn't told anyone but his brother. Paranoid thoughts about who ratted him out were rushing through his brain and he thought, *I'm fucked.*

Captain Ortega had quickly put together the multi-agency task force to get Green after Chico had told him about the warehouse directly behind Cosmo Green's office. Chico had once managed the warehouse operation, which was a non-profit put together by Cosmo called "Lightly Used."

The warehouse was organized into sections for bicycles and motorbikes, tools and landscape equipment, electronic devices like TVs and sound equipment, musical instruments, and household appliances. On the surface it was a jobs program that hired people to refurbish items that were purchased at auction or donated.

However, Chico had told them that it was mostly

a large fencing operation that bought stolen items at pennies on the dollar from drug customers known by the Beastie dealers. Some of these customers also worked in the warehouse removing license plates and registration numbers and were paid in drugs. They took most of the refurbished altered products to swap meets in the Bay Area from Marin to San Jose where they brought top prices and were unlikely to be seen by their former owners. They also laundered a lot of cash through the non-profit.

Chico had suspected there was a tunnel between the law office and the warehouse that Maurice would disappear into at times. He knew for sure Maurice had an escape route in case of a raid. The warehouse was only one of several buildings owned by Maurice and managed as a front by his brother. They also ran a massage parlor, an auto body shop, two twenty-unit apartment complexes, and part interest in a card parlor, as well as Golding's check cashing business.

Captain Ortega's team had scanned the Green properties with the latest technology and they discovered the tunnel underground between the buildings. When they'd followed Golding and Amos Brown to Cosmo

Green's office that morning they suspected that Maurice would also meet with them. They obtained the necessary warrant, and hit the jackpot when they found the fencing operation in the warehouse next to Cosmo's office and of course Maurice Green himself.

The Task Force had also staked out Cosmo Green's office, which they knew to be heavily fortified. They watched as Amos Brown and Golding came out and two of them followed Golding in an unmarked car. They waited and about a half hour after they'd grabbed Maurice, Cosmo walked out his front door and was also arrested.

Their welders were still working on the large vault they had found. They hoped to find a lot more cash and incriminating documents and, if they were really lucky, a serious cache of drugs. They were busy matching items in the warehouse to lists of stolen goods at the police station. Ortega's task force high-fived each other back at their FBI meeting knowing that this was just the tip of Maurice Green's criminal iceberg.

Ortega called the head of the protection detail assigned to Chico who had been moved out of town only the day before. "Hey Bud, tell our guy his information has been golden and we've got the perp and his brother in custody on a whole host of charges. If we're lucky we may have enough to put them away without his testimony. Either way now the feds will fund and staff his witness protection and relocation."

Ortega then called Sam to let him know that they had Green in custody. Again he thanked him for his help. Sam was relieved, having lost some sleep worrying about whether he and Sheila would be safe from retaliation. He'd received a threatening letter just the day before in the mail:

YOU ARE A DEAD MAN!
YOU WON'T LAST LONG ENOUGH TO
SPEND THE STOLEN GOLD!

He had passed the letter to the police who were checking it for prints or another way to identify the sender, but so far they had nothing. Still, with Green and Golding both behind bars, Sam felt a whole lot safer.

Sam called Jake at New Life Wednesday afternoon to thank him for his role in getting Chico to talk to the cops and the resulting arrests.

"I'm glad they got the gang leaders, but now they need to get Paul's murderer," said Sam.

"I was just about to call you Sam," Jake said excitedly. "I've been talking to Jan Brown, Druggie Dave's ex-partner, who just got released from the mental health lock-up and into our program. Dave abandoned her after she got committed and she's pretty pissed off at him. Tony asked me to help her get acquainted with folks here and settled in. So we're talking and she's way less crazy than she used to be on the streets.

"Anyway, she tells me that Dave met with a guy his dealers brought over the afternoon before Paul and Charlie were shot. She thinks the guy gave Dave a bag with some money and other stuff and listen to this, Dave snuck away from their camp in the middle of that night and was gone a couple of hours."

"No shit, do you think she would recognize a photo of the guy who gave Dave the money?"

"Well, remember she was pretty out-of-it when this happened, but I think Ortega is going to want to talk with her anyway. I asked her if she would be willing to talk to police and she said she was. You think Dave could've killed Paul?"

I better run this by Tony, thought Sam. "Let me call Tony. If he's cool with it I'll call Ortega right away."

Sam first called Tony at Living Sober to explain what was happening. Tony wasn't thrilled—this was the second patient in only a few days to be pulled into a police investigation—but he wanted the murderers behind bars. He said he'd cooperate with the police.

As soon as he had Tony's permission, Sam called Ortega to tell him about the lead and explained that Jan was in the same program Chico had been in. He asked Ortega to go through Tony to set up an interview. Ortega said he would get right on it and asked Sam if he wanted to sit in.

Sam said, "I'm tied up this afternoon speaking at a forum on homelessness at Sac State."

About an hour later Ortega met with Jan Brown and Jake at Tony's office. Jan was able to identify Franklin Golding from his photo as the man who came to their camp with Dave's two regular dealers. She also identified the dealers from the mugshots of the Beasties.

"This guy"—she pointed at the photo of Golding—"stayed after the dealers dropped the crystal and he talked with Dave for a while. He and Dave walked to the guy's car and when Dave came back he was carrying a small duffel bag. Dave told me he was doing a job for the guy who'd paid him in cash."

Ortega asked, "Did you see the cash or ask Dave what the job was?"

"No, I saw the bag and Dave told me there was money. He said it was better if I didn't know what the job was."

"You also told Jake that Dave left your camp that night, right? Do you know what time he left or came back?"

"I know he was gone for a while, maybe a few hours. I don't know what the times were, but it was in the middle of the night."

"Did he say anything about it the next day? Did you ever see any of the money?"

"He acted weird the next day, but he didn't say a word about it and he hid the duffle bag somewhere. It wasn't in our tent or camp that I could find. A couple days later he said he'd take me shopping and he did, but that was when I got taken to the mental health center. I haven't seen or heard from him since."

"Do you have any idea where Dave might have gone?"

Jan thought for a moment. "We met up in Tehama and lived in trailer parks from there to Redding for a few years, he could have gone back there."

Sam was standing on the dais facing a crowd of over one hundred and fifty students and faculty. Beside him were several people who had made it out of homelessness. Their panel was introduced by John Pratt, a social work professor who had been a mentor to Sam when he was in graduate school.

Pratt announced, "Bill Buckmeister and Tom Wong from the Chamber of Commerce will be speaking on 'Homelessness from a Business Perspective' following this panel. I'd like to introduce a former student of mine, Sam White, who is the Co-Chair of the Sacramento City-County Homeless Board and Director of St. Francis Village."

Sam started, "Thanks for being here and for your interest in homelessness. I began my social work career in the late seventies, and I can tell you that we didn't have homelessness then as we have it today. Sure, there were many people with mental illness or addictions, but housing was more affordable. Between public housing and old SRO 'flop house' hotels, cheap housing was accessible to even the poorest people, and tens of thousands of severely mentally ill adults were living in state mental hospitals.

"Then came Ronald Reagan, who as California's governor released tens of thousands of mental health patients from state hospitals to save money. The problem is that he never adequately funded his promised community treatment programs, leading to an embarrassing number of mentally disabled people living on our streets or in our jails."

There were murmurs from the crowd. Sam couldn't tell if they were murmurs of approval or disagreement, though he hoped for the former. He exchanged glances with his fellow panelists and then pressed on.

"In the early eighties President Reagan shifted billions of dollars from public housing programs to the military budget. Us housing advocates knew this could lead to widespread homelessness within ten years. But combined with the loss of higher paying union jobs, urban redevelopment, recessions, and the disintegration of extended families, homelessness grew exponentially in only three or four years. We began to see hundreds of people on our streets here in Sacramento during Reagan's second presidential term."

Sam could see several members of the crowd nod

their heads as if suddenly making the connection between the time period and the skyrocketing homeless
rates. A few others looked lost. He could throw history
lessons at them all day, but he needed to connect the
crowd to the reality *now*.

"My point here," Sam said, "is to show that homelessness is caused by social and economic policies and these
are things we can change. Huge public housing projects
are difficult to manage effectively and tend to isolate
impoverished families in one area, but smaller housing
projects in scattered sites are better managed and more
fairly spread throughout neighborhoods. We also know
that even chronic homeless people who have multiple
disabilities can be successfully housed in subsidized
housing with supportive services."

One of Sam's fellow panelists spoke up on cue. "We
have a growing database demonstrating that providing
permanent supportive housing to homeless people with
disabilities saves money. These very sick people usually
bounce from the streets into expensive emergency programs, using up costly police, ambulance, jail, emergency
room, and mental health resources. With permanent
supportive housing we can end homelessness, plus save

lives and money in the long term."

A third panelist interjected, "You'll hear from Bill Buckmeister later that homeless people don't want housing, that they just want to be irresponsible winos and camp for free in our parks. I have surveyed hundreds of homeless people on whether they would accept housing if they could afford it and over ninety percent will answer, 'Of course! I want housing.'"

It was Sam's turn to speak once more. "At the Village in Dignity Park we have a memorial wall where we hold services for our departed guests. On average we hold a memorial service every eleven days, and these are just the homeless people who have come to use our services. Homelessness kills! Just today we had a memorial service for Paul Dixon who was murdered by thugs after finding the lost gold you may have read about this week. Paul and his campmate are truly the victims here, but the city and county response is to cite homeless campers and make them move deeper into the river parkway or into neighborhood parks and alleys nearby.

"There is something we can do about it! Whether you volunteer in our dining rooms to feed people or whether you lobby government to increase the supply of supportive housing there is something everyone can do to end homelessness.

"Please join in this effort, even a few hours a month can make a difference. A coalition of people and organizations lead by St Frances Village are currently sitting in the lobby of the County Board of Supervisors every day until the county board agrees to increase the number of shelter beds and housing for homeless families. At the end of an average day in our Dorothy Day Crisis Center we send between forty and fifty women and children out into the streets without shelter because we cannot find a place for them to go. This is unacceptable and we must change it. Please help yourself to our information on the table and visit our website <u>St.FrancisVillage.org</u>."

Franklin Golding limped out of Cosmo Green's office Wednesday morning with Amos by his side.

Golding whispered, "I'll pay you five hundred bucks to go to his house and fuck over that asshole Sam White." He handed Amos the cash and the address. Amos took it, nodded and walked away without a word. Golding climbed painfully into his Lincoln Navigator. He was seething.

Fucking Green talking to me like that. I could fuck him over ten different ways. That dick Sam White is going to pay too. I was so close to the gold. That fucker set me up to find it for him.

Golding had been in jail and missed the televised press conference about the gold being found, but he had read the paper and guys in the jail were talking about it. He remembered that he needed to send another flunky to drop off another missive to White on his way back to his high-walled, razor-wired compound. He'd already sent one threatening letter from the jail through Cosmo.

He was glad to be home after four nights in jail. His leg was killing him so he kicked back on his recliner chair to watch a Sopranos rerun. A minute into it his phone rang.

Golding was pissed—he didn't want to be interrupt-ed—but he answered it. It was Cosmo on the line.

Cosmo said, "Hey I'm sending a guy over later to deliver the file cabinet we discussed with organized receipts."

Golding answered, "No problem, thanks for taking care of that so soon." There was a click on the other end of the line. That suited Golding just fine; he didn't want to spend any more time than he had to talking to the slimy fuck.

Golding couldn't watch TV anymore. He spent the next hour considering his options. He thought, *I am not going back to jail or prison. Fuck no! If they come at me with the embezzlement charges or if the FBI starts climbing up into my shit, I'll post bail with my property as collateral and leave the country. I've got a lot of cash on hand, but I need to clean out my accounts.* Cosmo had helped him open an off-shore account too and he had about fifty thousand in there.

Golding couldn't help thinking about his rummy old man who had died with nothing but his small, rundown house not long after his mother passed. They had both died in their early sixties after years of drinking and fighting. He'd already outlived them and he was determined to live well on some island or South American country where his money would buy women and good food and comfort. He dreamed of himself on a tropical beach, a brown-skinned woman waiting on him, rubbing suntan oil on his back.

He had lived in North Sacramento his whole life, but he'd come to a decision.

"Fuck this place!" he bellowed. "I need to get out of here as soon as possible—like tomorrow!" He spent the next couple hours planning, packing and assembling his cash, clothes and valuables. His broken left ankle slowed him down, but at least he could drive. He would get the cast removed later. He had formulated a plan a while ago in case he had to split quickly.

He would dump his car for a new, unregistered one and drive straight to Tijuana, Mexico and then keep driving south to La Paz. From La Paz he could get another car and take it by ferry to Mazatlan.

Mazatlan would take him straight into mainland Mexico and across to the Yucatan and then he would charter a sailboat to take him to a Caribbean Island where they spoke English. He could probably sell the latest car in Mexico for cash.

Shit, but the Green brothers would be looking for him—did they have contacts that far south? Maybe he would just island hop and work his way south. Maybe they would be glad he left and they'd leave him alone. He had never been on a sailboat, but he'd always thought it would be a cool thing to do.

His fantasizing was cut short by the buzzer on his

gate. He looked at the monitor of his security cameras and saw a delivery man in uniform. A cap shadowed the man's face as he pushed a hand truck loaded with a big box. The buzzer sounded again and Golding limped down to meet the guy to let him in.

"Delivery to Franklin Golding," the man called out as he approached. "That would be me," Golding opened the gate, waved him to the back door of his office and let him inside.

He pointed for the cabinet to go next to a couple of others. The man opened the box and pulled out a deep five-drawer file cabinet. He slid it out of a large plastic bag, stuck the bag in the empty box and put it back on the hand truck. He handed Golding a receipt to sign.

Golding bent over to put the paper on his desk and began to sign it. Suddenly, he felt something thin and tight around his neck.

He struggled to get his fingers under the wire choking him, but he was too late. He felt the man's knee between his shoulder blades as his head was being bent back and his chest jammed into the edge of the desk. He felt pressure build around his neck, head, and chest as he gasped for precious air that just wouldn't come. He struggled for close to a minute, but the killer held on longer.

When the delivery man was certain Golding was dead, he folded and tied the still-warm corpse into a fetal position and stuffed it into the large plastic bag. With some difficulty he pulled the box down over the bound body. Then he righted the box, secured it with duct tape, and tipped it forward as he slid the hand truck under it. He walked out into the compound, continuing to keep his hat low and his head down. He went into the house, found the camera monitors and shut down the system. He looked at his watch.

"Right on time," he said to himself, then looked through the house for a suitcase to pack some of the dead man's things. He had been told to make it look like Golding had packed his valuables as if he wasn't coming back. When he got to the bedroom he hit the jackpot.

The fucking guy has already packed a bag of his things. There were big wads of cash, IDs, credit cards, phones and other valuables in a pile next to the bag. He stuffed everything into the bag,

"Shit! Must be tens of thousands," he said excitedly. He walked with the suitcase back into the office to get his package and left by the side gate. He put the box and large suitcase on a lift gate, then loaded them into his van. He drove off with a big smile on his face.

The two cops posted outside Golding's compound had been watching the delivery with interest. Golding had met him at the gate, but wasn't there as the delivery guy had come out. The big box looked heavier on the way out than it had on the way in—and he also had a large suitcase. What kind of delivery man left with a suitcase?

As the van backed up they quickly decided they should split up. One officer stayed behind to keep an eye on Golding's compound; Officer Bates got in their unmarked car and followed the van.

As Ortega left his meeting with Jake and Jan he made sure to thank Tony. He knew that this work was putting strain on the New Life residents, but unfortunately it had to be done.

Once outside he immediately called his surveillance team on Golding. "Bring Golding back in for questioning. He's suspected of conspiracy to commit murder."

"Sir," the officer responded, "I'm alone at the residence. I just called it in, but we had a delivery driver come to Golding's place, truck in a big box to Golding's office, then leave with what looked like the same box and a big suitcase. Bates left to follow the driver in our undercover car. Last I heard the guy was on the eighty freeway heading east and Bates plans to pull him over before he leaves the county."

"Okay, I'll send another unit as backup for you and when they arrive I want Golding in custody."

Meanwhile, Tony sat with Jake and Jan. He was especially worried about Jan, given how close she seemed to Dave.

"Are you sure you're okay, Jan? I'm concerned that this stuff might stress you out and your recovery should come first."

"Yeah, I'm good. I never thought I'd be ratting on Dave with the cops though. I'm so pissed at Dave and it felt good to get this off my chest. I'm worried about what he mighta done."

"You've barely started recovery and God knows you need some clean time. Let's leave the worrying to the cops now and get you back to the program," said Tony.

"Tony, wait," said Jake. "I want to tell Mota and Cat about this. They should know."

"Are you sure, Jake? Temptation is very strong

around old friends."

"I'm sure. I know I can handle it, Tony. And I bet I know right where they are."

"Let me get Jan settled with one of the staff, and I'll come with you. Then we're coming right back."

Jake didn't like the idea of Tony tagging along, but he needed to tell Mota and Cat about Jan and Dave. So once Jan was settled, Tony and Jake headed to Dignity Park.

———————————

Mota and Cat had just got word from Jake that Druggie Dave was wanted for questioning in Paul's murder. They were in Dignity Park, which was getting ready to close.

Cat spit, "Fucking A! We saw that asshole Dave just as he was leaving."

"We didn't even ask where he was going," Mota replied, shaking his head. "Let's go over to the woodpile and ask around. The meth heads might have heard something, some of them were Dave's customers."

They found that most of the woodpile had moved on already but Big Mama was still there. She was the de-facto leader of the clan. She was bad news and dealt crystal herself; her brawny sons were barely adults but they did her dirty work. She was a big woman. Her teeth were gone and her cheap dentures gave her puckered face a weird frown.

She saw them approach. "What the fuck do you want?"

Cat had been an off and on customer, so she knew Big Mama better than Mota. "We come in peace Big Mama. We just found out that Druggie Dave is wanted for questioning in Tinker's murder. We saw him pack up his camp and we haven't seen him since. We wondered if you'd heard anything about where he went. He left Jan behind at the mental hospital."

"Nothing that fucker did would surprise me. Jan was crazier than a bed bug, but Dave was sly. As long as he stayed on the island and made folks come to him I left him alone, but if he came into my territory he knew we'd fuck him over. How would I know where the fuck he's gone?"

"We hoped you may have heard something through your network."

Big Mama did a body chuckle but her frowning face never smiled. "My fucking network. Give me a break." Still, she lowered her voice a couple notches and said,

"We mostly got our crystal from the same source and I heard they're lookin' for Dave too. He took off without paying his debt. They tracked him by bus up to Redding, but they haven't found him yet. I talked to my guy yesterday, but you didn't hear a fucking thing from me, am I right?"

Cat and Mota thanked her profusely for her info and assured her of their confidentiality. Neither of them were willing to double-cross Big Mama.

She looked at them coldly. "The same dealers were asking if I'd heard anything about a bunch of homeless fucks that ambushed their people with slingshots or some such bullshit. I heard a rumor. You two wouldn't know anything about that would you?" Without waiting for an answer, she turned away and waddled out of the Park.

They went to a pay phone and tried to call Sam, but he didn't answer. They searched for Captain Ortega's card and finally located it. Both of them would rather talk to Sam, but they didn't have time to wait. Who knew how long it would be before Druggie Dave took off again?

It took a while for his secretary to track him down, but he eventually answered, "Hello, this is Captain Ortega."

"Hi Captain this is Cat, uh Oretha Johnson calling about Paul Dixon."

"Hi Cat, I remember you. What can I do for you?"

"Well, Mota, uh Moreno and I heard that you may be looking for Druggie Dave, I mean Dave Brown. We saw him the day he was packing up to leave, which was Saturday. He didn't say where he was going, but we just found out from someone who would know that his dealers are looking for him. They've tracked him by bus to Redding. They haven't found him yet as of yesterday, but we thought you should know this."

"Thanks for calling Cat, this helps."

"Glad to help out Captain. I hope you find him soon."

"If you guys hear anything else, don't hesitate to call and ask for me."

As soon as he got off the phone with Cat, Ortega called his old colleague who was now an Assistant Sheriff for Tehama County. After they caught up, he told him about the case and that Dave Brown probably arrived by bus at Redding either Saturday or Sunday. He said he'd be sending a couple of officers to help track Dave down and his contact offered cooperation from the Sherrif's Department.

Ortega then got a call from his officer at the Golding compound. "We got no answer Captain, so we went in and Golding is gone. We've looked everywhere. Unless he has some secret tunnel out of this complex, he must have gone out with the delivery driver in the box."

Just then a radio call came in from Officer Bates. "This is 1029 in pursuit of a blue delivery van. I attempted to pull the subject over as he exited the 80 Freeway at the Marconi off-ramp, but he ran a red light. He's heading north on Marconi over Roseville Road at about seventy miles per hour."

Ortega could hear the officer's siren blaring in the background. Two other cars called in to say they were in the area and would join the pursuit. Ortega asked about helicopter backup and was told they would be fifteen minutes out.

On Marconi, Officer Bates drove seventy miles an hour a half block back from the van—but the van showed no sign of slowing down. It flew through the Del Paso intersection despite the red light, avoiding a crash by some small miracle.

Suddenly up ahead, a black and white flew around the corner of a side street just as the van hit the intersection and they sideswiped each other. The police car ricocheted into a nearby parked car as the van swerved wildly, narrowly missing an oncoming bus.

"Officer Roberts," radioed Officer Bates, "do you copy? Are you injured?"

For a brief second, there was no reply, and Officer Bates feared that the man in the other police car had been hurt—or worse.

Then: "This is Officer Roberts, continue pursuit, I'm okay."

Officer Bates breathed a sigh of relief. "Copy that. Suspect vehicle is smoking badly and has now come to a stop. Vehicle is badly damaged, from the looks of it we're gonna need an ambulance."

The van, its right side caved in, had slowed at the next cross street and swung left in front of oncoming traffic. The driver looked back at Bates and fired a pistol.

Bates braked just as his windshield spider-webbed and a bullet whizzed past his right ear.

"Shots fired, I repeat, we have shots fired!"

Bates couldn't turn left without causing another crash. His only option was to stop in the left lane with cars going by in both directions. He stopped just in time to see the rear of the van get clipped by a beer truck and spin out of control across the center lane of the cross street into an oncoming garbage truck.

Crunch!

The van was crushed and twisted, smoke billowing from both ends. When Bates was able to turn left he stopped behind the van, climbed out of his unmarked Ford, and approached with his gun drawn. He peered into the van window to see the driver's legs crushed between the seat and console and his head over the steering wheel, part way through a misshapen wind shield. He was unconscious and bleeding heavily from his face and legs.

Chapter Ten – Closure

Wednesday, April 17, 2002

After the Wednesday evening AA group at New Life, Jake sat down with Skip, a local musician who fronted for a popular blues band. Jake had a lot of respect for someone who got clean living that life and trusted his advice even when it wasn't what he wanted to hear.

"I know I only have about a week in recovery, but I wanted to talk to you about trying to reconnect with my family."

His sponsor knew his story and paused to consider how to respond. "Well, you're on like steps one and two right? You've been gone from your wife and son for almost two years. How long do you think you need to be sober before they take you seriously?"

Jake's throat felt tight and tears filled his eyes. Eventually he croaked out, "A lot more than a week, I guess."

He tried to compose himself, but the tears were flowing now. "Now that I'm clean the pain just overwhelms me sometimes. I miss my wife and son and daughter so much. I can't get my daughter back, but my wife and son are so close—I miss them so much! I've fucked things up so bad that I'm afraid they won't want to see me and I don't know if I can handle that."

Skip reached out and put his hand on Jake's shoulder. "You can't change what's already happened and you can't control other people's reactions. All you can do is stay clean in this moment and learn to live with the pain. You've made some difficult decisions and are on the path to recovery; you need to stay clean, work the steps and the program, and try not to be too attached to the outcomes. Trust that if you take care of yourself and your recovery other things will fall into place. Some of the steps ahead will be extremely tough. How about when you have a month in, we come back to this and see what we think?"

Jake wiped his face and shook his head. "Sounds good, thanks."

Thursday, April 18, 2002

Late Thursday morning Druggie Dave sat in his newly rented trailer in a space at the Old Oaks Camp and Trailer Park south of Redding. He was looking out his window through dingy orange curtains on a thin green lawn shaded by an old oak. The tree towered over the park owner's trailer and small reception building at the front of the park. Lucky, his pit bull, was laying by their front door.

Dave was high on crystal, his breath shallow, beads of sweat on his forehead, TV droning in the background. He did a double take as a young Asian man in a sweatshirt and baseball cap approached the office.

He jumped up yelling, "Shit! Shit!" He recognized the guy immediately as one of the Beasties he'd dealt with in the past. He was glad he'd paid the owner a nice chunk of change to accept his alias without an ID and to deny he was there to anyone that came asking.

He quickly pulled his curtains closed but peeked out an upper corner. The guy walked out a few minutes later and looked at his trailer and others nearby. Instead of walking away, he turned into the park and walked down the main footpath through the lines of trailers on either side. He walked past and Lucky started to growl.

Dave whispered, "Shut up!" and hunched by the door close to the dog. *What the fuck is he doing?* he thought.

The Beastie approached a gray-haired woman on her porch a couple of trailers down and started to talk to her. *What if he's asking if she's seen any new tenant that looked like me?* He fought an urge to run out the back, get on his old motorcycle and take off.

Just then the park owner hurried down the path and yelled to the guy, "Hey you can't just walk through here and bother the residents! You need to go."

"What are you going to do, call the cops?" The guy laughed. "I'm just talking to this nice lady." The older woman just turned away and slammed her front door behind her without saying a word. The guy walked past the owner and Dave heard him say, "If I find out you're lying to me I'm going to kick your ass."

"I've already called the cops they should be here any minute," the owner lied. As the Beastie walked away Dave groaned with relief, popped the top on a cold beer and sat back on his tattered couch.

He thought as he laid out his rig on the coffee table. *I just have to lay low for a while longer and those fuckers will give up. Maybe I should've just paid them everything I owed. At least I have a real bed to sleep on and a roof over my head.*

The trailer park was laid out on a ridge that overlooked a bend in the Sacramento River. Though it was well beyond its prime, it was a nice spot. He had never been able to afford a park like this last time he was here.

I had to kill the deaf bum for it, he thought, *but I'm rid of Jan and I got a new start.*

"Fuck," he said out loud. "It was way easier than Golding promised. Didn't even have to look the bums in the face—and it sure as fuck paid off. Cops won't find the gun in the river anyway."

Now feeling reassured, Dave completed his ritual by poking the needle into the scarred vain on the back of his hand and pushing down the plunger.

———————————————————

Captain Ortega had sent detectives O'Toole and Diaz from his homicide squad to Tehama County late afternoon Wednesday to track down David Brown. The Tehama County Sheriff's office had agreed to cooperate.

They had a police mug shot of Brown after a drug arrest in Tehama a few years earlier. They had questioned a host of staff at the bus station and now they were targeting cheap motels and trailer parks.

They'd been at it since last night with no results. It was late afternoon on Thursday when they parked in front of the Old Oaks Trailer Park. They entered the tiny reception office and saw an unshaven man of about sixty with stringy gray hair. He was wearing a San Francisco Giants jersey and baseball cap and watching his team play on a small television that set on the counter.

The officers flashed their badges.

Sergeant Diane Diaz took the lead. "We're with the Sacramento Police Department, Homicide Division and we're looking for this person, David Brown." She pushed the photo across his countertop.

The man was still watching the game. After the pitch he looked down at the photo and there was David Johnson, the guy he had just rented a trailer to in the last week.

Shit, he thought, *this guy has become really bad news.*

The police officers were still looking at him expectantly. The owner carefully raised his eyes to meet

Sergeant Diaz's gaze.

"He told me his name was Johnson. Has he done something bad?" The two detectives looked at him with renewed interest.

"You know this man?" snapped Diaz.

"Well, uh, I might," he whispered. "It looks like the new resident who paid me a bunch of money to say he ain't here, but I ain't gonna lie to no cops. There was another guy here this morning looking for him and he was trouble. This Johnson rented the trailer across the lawn, number three there." He pointed out his side window. "He may be out. I saw him drive off on his old motorcycle about an hour ago. He's barely left his trailer in the last five days since he moved in. Probably went off for food. He's got a pit bull in his trailer you know. What is it he's done?"

"He's wanted for questioning in regards to a homicide." O'Toole got a description of the motorcycle. "Do you know if he's armed?"

"I have no idea."

"We're going to pull our car into your park behind this other row of trailers and wait for him to come back. Do you have a problem with that?"

The owner shook his head no. He didn't want to get into any legal trouble. "You do whatever you need to do, but I have a lot of seniors staying here, so be careful."

Dave rode in on his old Yamaha 150 at about five. He had two big Jack in the Box bags, a six pack and a sack of dog food stuffed into a basket bungeed to the back of his seat.

"He just rode in," reported Diaz on the radio to local deputies. "We'll wait until he is off the bike then try to rush him before he can make it into the trailer. If he gets into the trailer we will wait for your backup. He may be armed and we don't want to deal with his pit bull."

"Roger that, we got a unit on the way," came the voice of a deputy.

Diaz and O'Toole quietly climbed out of their car, leaving the doors ajar. Hands on their holsters, they crouched low darting behind trees and trailers. Brown was on the small wood-planked porch, almost to the front door so they broke into a sprint.

They charged across the lawn, drew their weapons, and yelled, "Police! Stop where you are and kneel down!"

Dave freaked. He lunged to his front door and though he tried to pull his key out and get it to the lock, his head and shoulders hit the door first and he crumpled to the tiny porch where the officers quickly cuffed him. Lucky growled and barked inside.

"My neck, my neck!" Dave screamed, though he was wriggling all parts of his body and craning his head around to see what they were doing.

"Why did you run for the trailer dumb shit?" scoffed Diaz.

"You have the wrong guy," yelled Dave. "I don't know what this is about."

O'Toole responded, "We have a warrant for your arrest in the murder case of Paul Dixon. We are Sacramento Police Homicide detectives Diaz and O'Toole"—they flashed their badges. "We will be taking you to the local Sheriff's station for questioning."

"Shit, this is some big mistake." Dave yelled again, but the officers were already patting him down and reading Dave his rights.

A siren had been approaching and a Sheriff's Department black and white Crown Victoria pulled into the park. They put Dave, still handcuffed, in the back of the Sheriff's car. Then they called animal rescue to deal with the pit bull.

In the bleak gray interrogation room at the station, the officers turned on a handheld tape recorder and O'Toole reminded Dave of his rights.

"I got nothing to hide," he responded.

"Are you waiving you're right to legal representation?"

Dave nodded.

"We need you to answer verbally, yes or no," Diaz insisted.

"No I don't need a lawyer, Yes, I waive my right."

Diaz pushed a photo of Franklin Golding toward him across the metal table top. "Do you know this person?"

Dave glanced quickly at the photo and thought, *Shit! They already know about Golding.* The cops noticed his hesitation. "I've never seen this guy."

"That's funny," said Diaz, "because we have a witness who swears that you met with him at your camp." They saw panic flash across his eyes, followed by understanding.

He recovered quickly. "If your witness is my wife she is crazier than shit and I've left her because I can't take her drugging and blathering anymore. She'd say anything to get back at me and nothing she says makes any sense anyway."

Diaz pushed back. "We didn't say who our witness is, but they are ready to testify that this man Franklin Golding met with you and gave you money to do some work for him the afternoon before Paul Dixon was shot and killed. Did he give you money and a gun to kill Paul Dixon?"

Dave countered, "I don't know what you're talking about. My wife was so high she didn't know what the fuck was going on. Good luck with her testifying to anything that's believable."

"You are the only person naming your wife, Mr. Brown," Diaz said. "Why did you leave Sacramento a few days after the shooting and why are you using an alias here?"

"I left her and I don't want her to find me. Everyone who knows her knows she is crazy—just ask around!"

"We're going to require you to take a blood test because we saw you riding your motorcycle and your pupils are extremely dilated. We suspect you are under the influence. Then we're going to get a warrant to search your trailer for drugs and weapons."

"Look, I don't know nothing about this murder, but

I do want a lawyer if you're gonna start accusing me of other shit."

"We were discussing your drug use, Mr. Brown, but if you want to bring the topic back to the homicide we can discuss that."

Dave shut his mouth and refused to answer more questions. The officers retreated for now to contact a lawyer for Dave.

Later that evening they were all back in the same room. A public defender was present to represent Dave this time and a local Sheriff's Captain named Blood was now in the lead.

Blood started, "Well, based on your blood test which was positive for methamphetamine, we are charging you with driving under the influence of narcotics and we gained a search warrant for your trailer." Blood passed the warrant across the table to the attorney. "We have found over an ounce of crystal meth and thirty-five hundred dollars in cash in your possessions, would you like to comment?"

"My client has no comment," the attorney quickly replied.

"Well, we are also charging your client with felony

possession of illegal narcotics with intent to sell. Your client is wanted for additional questioning regarding a homicide in Sacramento County."

"I told you I don't know shit about that," Dave blurted angrily before his lawyer could cut him off.

The lawyer placed his hand on Dave's shoulder. "We have no comment at this time. I need to confer with my client in private."

At the lawyer's request, Dave was transferred to a different room; neither Dave nor the lawyer wanted to risk being recorded in the interrogation room.

"What is going on with this murder? I need to know to be able to protect you," the lawyer asked Dave when they were alone.

"My wife is in a mental hospital in Sacramento and she accused me of being involved with the murder of a homeless guy. It's been in the news."

"Yes, I've read about that. What's your involvement?"

"I'm not involved," yelled Dave. "My wife is pissed I left her and she's trying to fuck with me, that's all."

———————————

When Sam got home Thursday evening he found another threatening note in his mail.

YOU ARE A DEAD MAN!

THE GOLD YOU STOLE WILL HAUNT YOU.

YOU WILL BE SORRY YOU EVER LAID EYES ON IT!

He immediately called Ortega to tell him about the threat.

"I think Golding may have been your letter writer and he's out of the picture now, but I'll send someone over to get the letter and we'll process it."

"Out of the picture?" Sam asked. "What do you mean?"

"Golding's been found dead. I can't share the details just yet because we're still investigating, but it's safe to say that he won't be bothering anyone anymore."

Sam whistled. "I can't believe it. Can't say I'm sorry, though."

"Me neither," admitted Ortega. "Let me know if the threats continue. Do you want police protection?"

"No. I think you're right about Golding being the writer," Sam agreed. "With him dead and Green in jail I think I'll be okay. You don't think Green knows about the part I've played in his arrest do you?"

"No way!" said Ortega confidently.

Sam let out his breath. "Thanks for keeping me in the loop Captain."

"Hey, without you and Paul's friends we'd be dead in the water. Thanks for trusting us."

Ortega was reclining on the sofa in his office that night when his superior, Assistant Chief Burrell, pushed through the half-closed door.

"You've had quite a day, Ortega. From your report it looks like three different cases finally fell into place. That must feel awfully good, huh?"

"Yeah, I was just thinking about how you plod along on some cases and they never come together, but some days things just slide into place. In all honesty we had a lot of help from Sam White and some campers from the Village."

"Well, the Chief sends his 'atta boy.' He's a happy guy with Maurice Green and his brother behind bars. He said he's gotten pressure from council members to back off the river sweeps, so he's pulling us out of that for now."

"Good," Ortega sighed. "We got lucky on the murder-for-hire guy. He's in a coma and we caught him with Golding's dead body, the murder weapon and thousands in cash. He tried to make it look like Golding was absconding, but our guys were at the house and did some smart work. I just know that Green set up the hit. If we can tie him to that he's going down for the rest of his life."

Burrell responded, "Good, so the theory on the homeless killing is that Golding paid this Brown guy to shoot the poor campers to keep them from going back for the rest of the gold?"

Ortega said, "Yeah, now that we've got Brown in custody we'll sweat him. He doesn't know that Golding was killed, but so far he's denying involvement and there's still no murder weapon. We're checking the cash we found in his trailer for Golding's fingerprints."

———————————

Mota and Cat had moved deeper into the jungle north of the river to escape the police sweeps. Most of the Odd Squad and a couple others had moved with them to the same general area. They'd had their own wake for Paul with the usual drinking and reminiscing the night before. Captain Ortega had gotten word to them today that Golding had been killed and the head of the Beasties had been arrested.

Now as darkness settled into their camp they laid in

their tent on their bedrolls and passed a joint back and forth.

"What a roller-coaster week this has been," said Cat after blowing smoke. "I'll never forget finding Tinker and Charlie shot and how low I felt, but then finding out about Paul's gold and defending it from those assholes was such a high point. Then we lose Jake, but you and I get together." She looked into Mota's eyes and looked very vulnerable. "I'm starting to understand what they mean about silver linings. I know you miss Jake, but are you good with me being here?"

Mota looked at her and smiled warmly. "I'm better than good being with you babe." He held her hand and she smiled back. "Jake and I are close, but you know I wasn't really drinking so much before I met Jake. He was funny and has a heart of gold where others are concerned, but he was bent on self destruction. I was directionless and was easily sucked into his deathwish. I'm glad he's on a better path and I'm looking forward to slowing down on the drinking and drugging."

"Yeah, I know what you mean. I've been binging all week and I swore to myself that I would never be like those folks in the woodpile. Let's cut the hard shit all together, I don't want to support assholes like druggie Dave and Big Mama."

"You know, I heard you sing Amazing Grace yesterday and I was blown away. You've got soul sister! It made me want to go get my guitar out of storage and make some music."

"Damn right I'm a soul sister," Cat replied. "I used to sing in our church choir and I can play a little bass too."

"You're shitting me!" Mota was excited. "I'm gonna get my guitar tomorrow and we can start playing together. I might be able to find a bass for you too. I've heard there's a church in the North area that is storing instruments and letting campers play in their little hall every Tuesday. I haven't wanted to play since our band broke up and my wife left, but hearing you at the memorial, the spirit came back to me."

They kissed and started to take off each other's clothes. Cat said, "I can do all kinds of things with my mouth." She moved her way down to Mota's belt and zipper, her knees between his legs and he rolled his head back in pleasure, his right hand on the back of her head.

When she came back up he slowly rolled her over and swung around so he could unbutton her pants and their mouths pleasured each other with legs sticking out at either end. They both moaned deeply as crickets chirped and traffic hummed from the Garden Highway.

———————————————

Sam woke to Kabu's deep bark, which usually meant that raccoons or possums had come by to drink from their pool. Kabu was on her bed in the great room where she could look through the large sliding glass doors onto the back yard.

Sam in a sleepy voice said, "It's okay, Bu." But then she started to growl. This got his attention. He glanced at the clock and registered it was three in the morning. Sheila was still asleep, so he carefully slipped out of bed and into his shorts and flip flops.

He walked into the great room and when Kabu saw him, her growl deepened into a menacing warning. He looked to the backyard, but saw nothing out of the ordinary.

Right when he turned away, out of the corner of his eye he saw the head of a hooded figure looking at him through the side window.

Hoping to scare away the man, he yelled, "The police are on their way!" Kabu charged to the side door as the intruder kicked in more of the glass panes in the upper half of the door. Glass shattered and the frame bent inward, but the door held.

Sam saw the attacker was the big Beastie from the night the gold was found. He grabbed his phone from the counter and punched the emergency police number. Someone answered just as the door was kicked again and more glass panes shattered inward.

He yelled, "Home invasion please send help!"

Sam grabbed Kabu by the collar and jerked her back to keep her out of the glass. The big guy reached in with his left arm to try to unlock the deadbolt, but it needed a key. Sam dropped his phone on the counter, let go of Kabu and took a quick step forward. He levered his two hundred and thirty pounds into a right hand jab through the gaping hole in the top of the door. It flattened the guy's nose and staggered him for a moment.

Then the big man shook it off, shifted a large knife from his right hand to his left and stabbed through the jagged space. Sam jumped back as the knife came within an inch of his nose and Kabu lunged and chomped on the guy's forearm. She cried in pain as glass on the floor peirced her paws and she released her grip. Sam grabbed the closest thing he could reach—an iron—and threw it, clipping the guy's shoulder as Sheila appeared from the bedroom with her pistol and yelled, "I am armed and loaded." Sam heard a siren and so did the intruder as he sprinted out of the yard and disappeared.

Friday, April 19, 2002

It didn't take long for campers and staff at the Village to hear that Druggie Dave had been arrested. Sam had let folks know that the city police were backing off the sweeps and that the DA was dropping charges on most of the folks who had been cited and refused to move. This was a huge relief for the campers; they had been so afraid they would lose the closest thing they had to a home, but for now it looked like they could stay.

Jake got word from Ortega that Golding had been killed and Dave was in custody and he passed this along to Jan Brown.

When she heard this she said, "You know he was a decent man when we met, but the drugs just dragged us down so low that we were barely human beings. It was all about the next high and we lost everything. Maybe he can at least get straight now. I'm so done with that life, I don't ever want to go back."

Jake nodded. "Me neither, we just got to stay sober one day at a time and try to get a life." He said this for his own good as much as hers.

A little later, Jake got a call from Sam. "Hey Jake, you hanging in there okay?"

"Yeah, I'm trying to work my steps and the program here, as we say. I heard they caught Paul's killers—glad that Paul is getting some justice! How is Charlie?"

"Charlie is healing pretty good, He won't ever see out of his left eye again, but his hearing is better and they've done some skin grafts to cover scars on his face. The bad news is he's been diagnosed with early onset Alzheimer's, but he'll be taken care of probably in a Board and Care home."

"That's awful," Jake said, then stopped and took a deep breath. He was trying to work on being more positive. "At least he's alive and will be cared for."

"Jake, I called to check in, but also because I got a call from your wife," Sam paused and he could hear Jake swallow. Jake's heart suddenly pounded in his chest.

"What did she say?" Jake asked weakly.

"She asked about you and I told her you were in recovery, but it's only been about a week. I think she had heard this already from your aunt. She's glad you're sober, but she doesn't want direct contact until you've got more recovery time in. She said your son sends his love, but she doesn't want him to be disappointed again, so she wants to move slowly on reestablishing contact."

"I don't know what to say," Jake whispered and paused as tears welled in his eyes. "I don't deserve it, but it gives me some hope. Thanks for passing this on Sam."

"Jake you're a good man and a leader if you can stay straight. After you've got a few months in, I want to talk to you about working here at the Village."

"Wow, really? I'm blown away. I'll do my best to stay straight. I'd love to work at the Village. Hey, you know I had a dream last night that my daughter was in the room with me. It was so real and she talked to me." Tears welled anew. "She said, 'I'm sorry Daddy. I love you and miss you, but don't worry about me.'" He paused and swallowed painfully. "Then she said, 'Take care of Mommy and Stevie.'"

Sam was taking his turn in the county supervisors'

lobby that afternoon. Pastor Don and Sister Julie had come in to meet with him.

Pastor Don began, "So we heard about your incident at home last night. How's the arm?"

Sam lifted his arm to display the full bandage wrapped around his forearm just below the elbow and said, "Ten stitches, no big deal, but my Bu girl is still limping from the glass in her feet. The vet says she got it all, so it won't be long before she'll be catching Frisbees again."

Sister Julie said, "How is Sheila taking it?"

"Well, she seems okay. The guy was lucky he ran off when he did, because Sheila came out with her little target pistol and was ready to use it. I've never really liked the gun in the house, but I have to say, I'm glad she has it handy now."

Pastor Don reported, "Things seem a lot less tense in the park today after the news spread about Paul's killers getting busted and by all reports the police have backed off the sweeps."

"That's great. Ortega told me they were going to ease off," said Sam. "Any reaction to the sit-in, Sister Julie?"

Sister Julie replied, "Even though we've only been

at this a few days, Carly said she's already gotten calls from the Director of Social Services. They're considering funding a move for St. Vincent's Inn to a much bigger space. They could more than double their capacity and accommodate up to one hundred beds for families. They also want Carly and I to go with them to look at some possible sites for the shelter."

"That's great news, Sister Julie. Hopeful for only our first week, but we know that talk is cheap, and getting a site approved for a shelter could be a big fight. Still it's good to hear there is movement already," said Sam.

Supervisor Regina and Danny Aguilar walked into the lobby and in passing the supervisor looked at all three of them, shook his head, and chuckled to Danny and walked off without saying a word to them.

Danny stopped and in a low voice said, "You know the Supervisors think you guys are laughable and wasting your time."

"Really?" Sam retorted. "You're the second staff member who's come out to say that today. Our fifteen-thousand supporters will get a letter from us over the weekend and start calling into your offices. Monday things are going to get busy here." He held up his thick, dog-eared copy of the Autobiography of Mahatma Gandhi. "Someone later simplified and paraphrased what Gandhi taught on the power of civil disobedience over oppressors; First they ignore you, then they ridicule you, then they fight you and then you win."

EPILOGUE

Six Months Later - October 19, 2002,
Caesar Chavez Park facing City Hall

Sam and the board and staff of the Village, along with hundreds of homeless guests and volunteers, had marched that morning from the Village to City Hall, to the county building and now the park. A makeshift stage had been set up along I Street. Kalen and Carly were there, as well as faith leaders and many other supporters.

Mota and Cat had been playing music together for months, joining jams and open mic nights at the Torch Club and other venues. They had put together a band called the "Sling Shots." They played now for the crowd in the park.

Mota smiled and Cat was radiant as she belted their own blues tune: "I got the blues this morning, cause I ain't got a dime." The crowd was digging it.

It was a quintessential October day in Sacramento,

with temperature in the high seventies and leaves floating down from the Elm and Sycamore trees. Jake was there wearing his green Village Staff hat proudly and his wife and son were there to support him. They watched him help set up lunch bags, interact with guests, and stop to enjoy his friends' music when he could.

He walked over to his wife and son and put his arms around them. "Thanks for being here." They smiled and he stood a little taller.

Jake had relapsed at one month into the program, but had quickly reentered and had worked hard to maintain his sobriety since May. He'd started work at the Village two months ago and had reunited with his wife and son just one month earlier. Every day was a struggle, but he was so thankful for what he had now that he was determined not to lose it. He'd gotten good feedback from staff at the Village about his work and he'd already managed to bring a number of old camper friends, including Lizard and Bandana, into the Living Sober program.

After the music, Sister Julie walked on stage and took the microphone. "St. Francis Village thanks you for being here today to celebrate the end of our sit-in at the county." The crowd clapped. "As you know we started this sit-in six months ago to increase housing and shelter for our women and children. Today, I'm happy to report that this winter St. Vincent's Shelter will be moving into a larger facility and will expand from forty to one hundred beds." More clapping and cheers. "The county is also funding two new housing programs for homeless families in the South area that will add over seventy-five units." Yells and hoots from the crowd. "Never forget, when we work together for the common good we can move mountains!"

Sam and Pastor Don then joined Sister Julie at the mic.

Sam started, "Let's hear it for the Sling Shots!" The band members waved to the cheering campers as they were packing equipment. "I would like to thank some special guests, Councilmember Kalen Jones and Carly Johnson." They both waved from the front of the stage. "Supervisors Davis and Ortega who were with us throughout this struggle"—they waved and were cheered—"and Supervisor Regina who couldn't be here today, but cast the deciding votes.

"I thank you all for being here, for your efforts during this fight, and for all you do to help others. Let me ask you, is it too much to demand that our most vulnerable people have a roof over their heads and a bed to sleep in?"

The crowd roared, "No!"

"I'm proud to live in a community that takes care of its most impoverished people. I'd also like to share more good news with you today. We've just learned that the gold found by Paul Dixon has been purchased from Paul's family by a philanthropist and gifted to Sacramento State University for an historic exhibit. Paul's family has decided to donate a large portion of their proceeds to St. Francis Village to build a new men's shower, laundry, and bathroom facility that we plan to open in the next six months."

There was raucous applause and cheers from the crowd. Pastor Don said a prayer of thanks, blessed the food, and announced that lunch was served.

After the rally Sam and Jake met with Mota, Cat, and most of the Odd Squad at Temple Coffee. Mota and Cat were staying in the garage of one of their band members. They were still smoking weed and drinking, but had slowed down considerably as their music and relationship had filled holes in their lives and given them purpose.

Gremlin's wiry red hair stuck out in several directions. He was still homeless and back on the river. His dog Jaws was tied to a tree in front of the coffee shop and walkers gave him a lot of room as they passed.

Bandana had gotten sober and into a housing program and was happy to be inside with winter approaching. He was cleaner than usual and still sported a black bandana.

Lizard was there and was now staying at New Life, but he was on a waiting list for a new veterans' housing program and hoped to be inside before it got too cold. His buddy Pit bull was in the hospital with end-stage liver failure and didn't have long to live. China and Jube were also there, still sober, working at the Village and had moved into a studio apartment in midtown.

"It's great to see you all together. Thanks for meeting," Sam started in and turned to Lizard. "I'm really sorry about Pit bull."

Lizard looked away, his eyes watering, and he nodded. "Yeah, you know he f-finally stopped d-d-drinking a couple months ago, but the d-d-doc said he'd already d-done too much d-damage."

Sam said, "Let's go see him after this." Everyone

nodded. "Charlie is in a nice board and care home and seems relatively happy, but his dementia is getting worse. I'm not sure he recognized me when I saw him last, but at least he's being cared for.

"I wanted to update you all on Paul's case. The cops are still sure that Golding hired Dave and gave him a gun to shoot Paul and Charlie. With Golding dead, no murder weapon found, and Dave still denying his involvement, the DA couldn't bring charges. You have probably heard that Dave got twenty-two months in Corcoran prison for drugs, right?" They nodded. "Well, we just got word that Dave was found dead in his cell a few days ago." There was silence as they looked at each other.

"What goes around comes around," said Cat and they all nodded.

"Captain Ortega tells me that the guy who killed Golding came out of his coma two months ago, but he's paralyzed from the neck down. The DA agreed not to seek the death penalty if the guy would roll over on Maurice Green and he did. Green and his brother were still locked up awaiting trial for money laundering and a bunch of other charges, but now he's facing conspiracy to commit murder. They've continued to deny him bail, and it looks like he's going down.

"Anyway, I wanted to thank you guys again for saving the gold and making sure that Paul didn't die for nothing." Everyone, even Gremlin smiled and they all felt a pride that had become more familiar and hopeful. "Paul's and his family's contribution will be recognized when we build the new men's washhouse, but we know this wouldn't have happened without your fearless efforts."

Lizard slapped Mota on the back and added, "The S-Sling Shots, I like that." They laughed. After finishing their coffees they all went to see Pit-bull.

The next morning was a Saturday. Sheila and Sam had Kalen, Carly, Mike, and Mike's wife Gloria over for breakfast and coffee. Sam was holding the Bee and reading the article about the lawyers finally settling who owned the gold and the donor stepping forward to buy it for the university. The article also mentioned Paul's family's donation to the Village.

"I'm going to curate the gold exhibit for the university," announced Mike. "I've found a photo of Michael O'Connor that I'll include with the photos I have of Paul and the tree. It looks like it will be displayed in the

CSUS library initially, but the university hopes to move it around to other venues in the community."

"It's kind of amazing that the gold will be displayed so close to where it was found," said Sheila. "I think the new men's washhouse is the perfect ending for this squatter's gold saga. It means both Michael O'Connor and Paul Dixon made a difference, even though they didn't live to see it."

Kalen added, "Hey, did you see the business section? One of Bill Buckmeister's corporations has been indicted for tax evasion."

"Let's hope he won't be so quick to call homeless people criminals," said Sam.

Kabu trotted over, dropped her slobbery dog Frisbee in Sam's lap and looked at him expectantly.

They all cracked up as Sam held the dripping Frisbee at arm's length and said, "Thanks Bu."

Acknowledgments

To author a book was at the top of my bucket list after retirement and Paula Brook, a Vancouver writer offered to lead a free weekly writing group through the winter in our small town of Loreto, in Baja California Sur, Mexico. Her generosity opened the door to writing for me and I am indebted to all the writer's of the Loreto (Escritores) Writer's Collective over the last six years. Thanks to Paula Brook, LeRoy Chatfield, Edward Nugent and John Gavares for reading my early drafts and providing feedback. Thanks to professional editor Sara Page who smoothed my rough edges. Special thanks to my wife Cecile Martin (poet and escritora) who read and edited all my drafts and put up with my stubborn resistance.

I send my love and thanks to all the caring staff and volunteers of Loaves and Fishes, Sacramento (an iconic interfaith non-profit that feeds and assists hundreds of homeless and hungry guests every day) and the Board of Directors who hired me to serve as their Executive Director in 1999. Lastly, I am indebted to the many people suffering from homelessness and disabilities I have had the opportunity to know and learn from over my career.

 *"Tim Brown is a shining example of the great good that can be accomplished by one dedicated and moral individual - his dedication and devoted efforts toward serving the most vulnerable members of the Sacramento Community have helped provide... homes to hundreds of chronically homeless people."*

Darrell Steinberg - Mayor, City of Sacramento

Timothy A. Brown earned a masters degree in Social Work from Sacramento State University in 1984 and is a licensed Clinical Social Worker. An expert on the community treatment of mental illness and addiction; as well as the causes and solutions to homelessness, he has published reports and given expert testimony to 20 Superior Courts, local governments and the California State Legislature. His writing is inspired by actual events drawn from his thirty-five years of experience as a street level organizer/activist and manager of innovative mental health and homeless programs in Sacramento, California.

A recipient of many community service awards, Mr. Brown delivered a Commencement Address to 600 graduates of the College of Health and Human Services, Sacramento State University in 2005 and was honored with a Lifetime Achievement Award by the National Association of Social Workers, California Chapter in 2011.

A member of the Loreto Writers Collective since 2012, his short stories were published in "Reflections by the Sea" in 2015 with Blurb. This collection of short stories is about the ex-patriot experience in Baja California, Mexico.

Made in the USA
Lexington, KY
02 October 2018